W9-BJD-512

"When I called you," Mr. Patton said to the coach, *"I wanted you to know the background. When I learned that you already knew, I wanted to meet you and tell you that Chris's mother and I support his playing basketball, but only if he is really able to overcome the memory of the accident."*

"I understand."

"If the fear—and that's what it is, fear—overtakes him, he's got to quit. I mean, instantly. We don't want to damage our son. What we want is for him to recover."

Coach Fulton nodded and thought he saw what was coming next.

"As his coach, you're the one who will see first if the specter of that accident is tearing him apart. You'll be the one with him, and the first one to see good signs or, heaven forbid, bad signs. And we will be counting on you to take the necessary action and to do so promptly."

"Of course."

Brian Patton leaned back and smiled suddenly. "Doug, are you still sure you want my boy on your team?"

PUFFIN BOOKS BY THOMAS J. DYGARD

THE REBOUNDER

THOMAS J. DYGARD

PUFFIN BOOKS

PUFFIN BOOKS
Published by the Penguin Group
Penguin Books USA Inc., 375 Hudson Street, New York, New York 10014, U.S.A.
Penguin Books Ltd, 27 Wrights Lane, London W8 5TZ, England
Penguin Books Australia Ltd, Ringwood, Victoria, Australia
Penguin Books Canada Ltd, 10 Alcorn Avenue, Toronto, Ontario, Canada M4V 3B2
Penguin Books (N.Z.) Ltd, 182-190 Wairau Road, Auckland 10, New Zealand

Penguin Books Ltd, Registered Offices: Harmondsworth, Middlesex, England

First published in the United States of America by William Morrow and Company,
1994
Published in Puffin Books, 1996

1 3 5 7 9 10 8 6 4 2

LIBRARY OF CONGRESS CATALOGING-IN-PUBLICATION DATA
Dygard, Thomas J.
The rebounder / Thomas J. Dygard.
p. cm.
"First published in the United States of America by William Morrow and Company,
Inc., 1994" — T.p. verso.
Summary: Doug Fulton, coach of the Hamilton High Panthers, is certain that transfe
student Chris Patton can lead the team to a championship, but a tragic accident has
made Chris decide to never play basketball again.
ISBN 0-14-037702-6
[1. Basketball—Fiction. 2. High schools—Fiction. 3. Schools—Fiction.] I. Title.
[PZ7.D9893Rg 1996] [Fic]—dc20 95-46222 CIP AC

Printed in the United States of America

For my granddaughter,
Sarah Elizabeth Dygard,
with love

CHAPTER

Coach Doug Fulton had this crazy fantasy that played through his mind at the beginning of each of his three years as basketball coach of the Hamilton High Panthers.

Maybe, he admitted to himself, it was his youth that allowed his fantasy to flourish each September, when the students appeared for orientation and the new school year began. After all, he was only twenty-five and just three years out of college, so he was still young enough to believe in a big, bright, beautiful future—in which anything was possible. Maybe later the fantasy would fade.

In the meantime, he would continue to dream—and hope—that by sheer luck, through a miraculous stroke of good fortune, he would meet a half dozen transfer students on opening day, all of them standing about six feet six inches tall, all of them wearing letter jackets from their previous high schools—all of them eager to play basketball for the Hamilton High Panthers.

It wasn't difficult to guess why Doug Fulton had this fantasy. Each year, before the first day of school, he would look over the roster of boys returning to Hamilton High for the new season. It was always a squad of small players. Good shooters, maybe. Clever dribblers, perhaps. Able passers and dependable ball handlers, possibly. Yes, there was the occasional tall boy, but he was always too slow, too uncoordinated, too inexperienced. The good ones were small. Always. And a winning team needed one or more players capable of going up onto the boards, then tipping in an errant shot or capturing the ball.

"Maybe," he would muse on the first day of school, "one of the companies in the industrial park west of town has transferred in a man who has a son who . . ." Or maybe, as the fantasy got crazier, six men with tall, muscular, talented sons.

But the fantasy did not turn into reality the first year, nor the second. Coach Fulton's first team, then his second, managed winning seasons, but only barely. The Panthers finished fourth both years in the eight-team Spoon River Conference of small high schools in western Illinois.

Coach Fulton pulled his Volkswagen into a parking place on the asphalt lot behind the school and got out. He waved across the lot at Mary Corliss, the administrative secretary, and walked toward the building. The weather on this early September morning was hot, and he wore neither a coat nor a tie for the registration and orientation sessions scheduled for the day.

The old fantasy danced through his mind as he pulled open the door, and he smiled. He held the door open for Mary.

"You seem very happy," she said as she walked past him into the building.

He followed her in. "A funny little private thought," he said as they walked along the corridor.

"Oh?"

"It'll go away by the end of the day," he said, and grinned at her.

They parted at the end of the hall. She turned left to head up the short flight of stairs leading to the main floor and the principal's office, and he turned right toward his small office off the gymnasium.

Passing the gym, he heard the sounds of people already gathered around the tables on the basketball court for registration and the scheduling of orientation tours for new students. He walked on toward his office.

He unlocked the door, swung it open, and switched on the light as he stepped inside. He hadn't been in here more than three times during the summer. Most of his summer was spent away from Hamilton, working as an instructor at first one, then a second, basketball camp. Working with the players at the camps was the closest he came to actually playing basketball these days, and he enjoyed it.

He walked around the desk, unlocked it, then seated himself in his swivel chair, put his feet up on the desk, locked his hands behind his neck, and stared into space. The opening bell of the school day had not sounded, and so the start of registration was still a few minutes away.

He could entertain his fantasy for a few minutes, if he wanted. Then reality would end it for another year.

Maybe, he thought, that's the way it will end. Each year, the fantasy will fade a little. Then, one year, it simply won't be here. It'll be gone.

The bell rang, and he swung his feet to the floor, stood, and walked out of his office toward the gymnasium.

He saw the boy across the gymnasium when he looked up from putting together a packet of information for the girl standing in front of him.

"Thank you," the girl said as she took the papers.

Coach Fulton said, "Yes, sure, you're welcome." But he wasn't looking at her when he spoke. He was looking past her, at the tall boy standing alone across the floor. The boy looked like he didn't know what to do next.

He was a stranger to Coach Fulton. Clearly, he was new at Hamilton High.

He was tall—six feet six inches, maybe six feet

seven. He was slender, but not skinny, with broad shoulders. He held a notebook in a large hand at his side.

He was wearing jeans, a bright red T-shirt, and sneakers.

He shifted his weight from one foot to the other, looking around. Then he took a few steps to his right. He walked with the gait of an athlete, moving easily and smoothly, almost flowingly—something not always present in tall boys, even athletes.

The coach frowned as he watched the boy move over to one of the tables and, apparently, ask a question. Then the boy began receiving packets of information.

A voice from in front of Coach Fulton said, "Pardon me."

Doug looked into the face of a girl standing across the table from him. He did not know her. Probably an arrival from one of the two junior high schools. "Sorry," he said.

By the next day, the first full day of classes, Coach Fulton was able to put a name, Chris Patton, to the tall stranger, thanks to Mary Corliss.

"When I first saw him, I thought, Now there's somebody Doug Fulton is going to like," Mary said with a laugh.

"He does kind of stand out," Coach Fulton said.

"Tower above is more like it," she replied.

"Where's he from?"

"A high school in Indianapolis. I don't remember which one. I can find out, if you like."

"Doesn't really matter. I was just curious. Is he a senior?"

"Yes." She grinned again. "You've got him for only one season."

Coach Fulton nodded.

"Funny thing, though," Mary said. "He didn't list basketball as an extracurricular interest."

"Oh? But surely..." Doug Fulton paused and frowned. "Football?" he asked, his heart sinking. The boy did have the physique of a tight end. If he played football, that probably ruled out basketball. Few boys tried both.

"No. No sports at all. School paper, yearbook, and drama." Mary grinned again. "I think that what we've got here is a very tall, muscular aspiring actor."

"Drama," Coach Fulton said. "The boy is an athlete. You can tell before he takes three steps."

"Maybe so," Mary said. "But he didn't list any sports." She paused. "Maybe he considers basketball an integral part of going to school—you know, the real reason for attending—and doesn't see it as an extracurricular activity. We've had some of those, you know."

"Umm."

During the first week, Doug Fulton saw Chris Patton several times, but always from a distance. He didn't want to hail the boy in the corridor and ask about basketball. For sure, he did want to ask him, but only under the right circumstances. A coach certainly might ask a likely looking prospect to try out for a team. But he always took care not to come across as begging or even overly eager. The coach's role was to make a suggestion, offer an opportunity—not issue any promises. If a coach wasn't careful, sometimes a boy would misunderstand the expression of interest. And no team needed a player who thought he was a special case in the eyes of the coach.

As luck would have it, Chris Patton was in a gym class run by the football coach, Otis Humphrey, instead of one of Coach Fulton's own gym classes. So, deprived of the opportunity to approach the boy casually, Doug went to Coach Humphrey.

"Yes, the boy is an athlete, all right," Otis Humphrey agreed. "It sticks out all over him. But we'd already had football sign-up by the time I saw him, and he never said anything about it. I assumed he was a basketball player. Matter of fact, he looks like one to me. What makes you think he's not?"

"Nothing. I'm just interested. You can understand."

Coach Humphrey smiled. "Sure," he said.

Just two weeks before the start of basketball practice, Doug got the opportunity he wanted to approach Chris Patton.

The coach was walking along the main-floor

corridor, near the principal's office, during the few remaining minutes of the lunch hour. The corridor was almost deserted. But there, standing in front of the bulletin board outside the administrative office, was Chris Patton.

Coach Fulton walked up to him. "Hello," he said.

Chris turned from the bulletin board and looked at Coach Fulton. "Hello."

Doug was sure that Chris knew who he was, but he said, "I'm Coach Fulton, the basketball coach."

The boy nodded. "Chris Patton," he said.

"You're new to Hamilton High."

"Yes."

"I hope you'll be coming out for basketball. We start in a couple of weeks."

Chris flushed slightly. He looked uncomfortable. Finally, he said, "No, not me. I'm not a basketball player."

Coach Fulton looked at him a moment, then said, "You sure do look like one. Ever give it a try?"

"I'm not a basketball player," Chris said again.

The bell ending the lunch period rang, and Chris Patton literally fled down the corridor.

CHAPTER

2

The next morning, during his open period, Coach Fulton walked into the school's administrative offices. He spotted Mary at her desk, and she nodded to him. He glanced to his left, into Mr. Osborne's office, and saw the principal, his back to his desk, facing the window. He was holding the telephone receiver to his ear.

Coach Fulton walked around the counter and across to Mary's desk. "Can you look up the name of the high school in Indianapolis that Chris Patton attended?"

"Sure." Then she stopped and looked up at him. "What happened?"

"I introduced myself to Chris in the corridor yesterday and asked if he would be coming out for basketball."

"So?"

"You would have thought that I had asked him to burn down the town hall or something."

"What did he say?"

"Actually, it wasn't so much what he said. All he said was that he wasn't a basketball player. It was the way he acted."

"Maybe he was telling you the truth—he isn't a basketball player, just isn't interested."

"C'mon. He's not just big. He's an athlete. He shows it in a dozen ways. You said yourself that he was a boy I'd be interested in. You never said that about Timothy Wilson. Timothy is tall, but he's no athlete."

"How did Chris act?"

"He was flustered, embarrassed, and he virtually ran away from me when the bell rang."

"Umm. Well, over here," she said, leading him to a row of file cabinets against the opposite wall. She pulled open a drawer and muttered, "Patton, Patton," as she thumbed through the folders. "Here it is, Christian—not Christopher—Patton." She handed him the folder.

"Is there someplace I can sit?" Coach Fulton knew the rule against taking a student's file out of the administrative office.

Mary led him back to her desk, and he took a seat alongside it. He opened the file and riffled through the pages. "Hall High in Indianapolis," he said. Then he lifted another sheet and frowned.

"What is it?"

"He played junior varsity basketball in the tenth grade. Then he played on the varsity team in the eleventh grade but quit early in the season and did not letter."

"There's nothing unusual about that. A lot of boys go out for a sport and then change their minds. They don't like the hard practices, or they find something else that interests them more, or, like Timothy Wilson, they discover that they're not very good at the game."

"Uh-huh," Coach Fulton said softly, still frowning.

During lunch in the school cafeteria, Doug located Mrs. Harper, the English lit teacher, and asked her if she would mind giving up her free period to sit in for him in the one o'clock study hall. "It's important—sort of an emergency—and I have to leave the school for an hour," he said.

"I hope it's nothing serious," she said, peering through her glasses at Doug. She appeared genuinely concerned.

"No, no," Coach Fulton said. "Nothing like that. But it's important. I'll repay you with one of your study halls."

"There's no need for that," she said, and he knew she meant it.

Then Doug drove to his apartment.

He took the telephone off the desk, carried it across to an overstuffed chair, and sat down. He paused for a moment, holding the telephone on his lap, staring into space. Mr. Osborne was not going to like this, if he ever found out. Well, that was why Doug was here in his apartment making the telephone call. That way, Principal Osborne would not see — and question — a toll call to Indianapolis by the basketball coach. Nor would he be prompted to say that the call bordered on harassing a boy who had said he did not want to play basketball. Mr. Osborne seemed to view all athletics suspiciously and was especially cool to those who coached the sports. Otis Humphrey had warned him about the principal's attitude toward athletics on his first day, and Coach Fulton had seen hints of it on his own from time to time. No, Mr. Osborne would not be sympathetic.

But something in Chris Patton's manner left Doug convinced he was making the right move, no matter what Principal Osborne might say.

He lifted the receiver, dialed long-distance information, and asked for the number of Hall High, in Indianapolis.

Three minutes later he heard a deep voice saying, "Yes, this is Coach Barnes."

Coach Fulton, now hunched forward over the phone in his lap, explained who he was, why he was calling, and what he wanted to know. Then he stopped talking and waited.

There was a long moment of silence on the line.

Then Coach Barnes said, "It was a great tragedy."

Coach Fulton lifted an eyebrow and waited again.

"I'm sorry to hear that Chris is still carrying the burden of it. But I'm not surprised. I was hoping that the change of scene—with his father's transfer coming as it did—would enable Chris to leave it all behind him. But I never really believed it would happen. No, I'm not surprised."

Again Coach Fulton waited, but this time his mind was racing ahead with questions. Had Chris Patton been in some kind of trouble? Drugs, maybe? Or violence of some sort? A robbery? Doug realized that he knew nothing about Chris Patton. Was he opening something that was better left closed?

"Let me tell you what happened. But first, I want to say that Chris Patton is one of the best basketball players I've ever seen in more than twenty-five years of coaching, and he's a fine young man."

Coach Fulton nodded unconsciously. That did not sound like drugs or violent crime.

"He injured a boy in a scramble for a rebound. They were both going up for the ball. Chris turned quickly, trying to put himself between the ball and the other player. All of it was perfectly normal, except that his elbow came around like a trip-hammer and hit the other boy in the eye. A freak accident. Wouldn't happen again in a hundred years. Nobody's fault, really."

"The boy was blinded?" Coach Fulton asked.

"For a time," Coach Barnes said. "For a time it seemed he was permanently blind in the one eye. It was during this period that Chris decided he couldn't play basketball anymore. Later, with surgery, the boy recovered most of his sight. But for Chris, the damage had been done."

"I see," Coach Fulton said. He'had a vague recollection of hearing this story at one of the basketball camps over the summer. The story of the accident, so farfetched, was making the rounds in coaching circles. It had meant little to Coach Fulton at the time, not knowing either of the boys involved.

"Even the boy who was hurt—and his parents, too—didn't blame Chris," Coach Barnes continued. "They saw it for what it was—an accident, a freak accident. But Chris took all the blame on himself. The guilt just ate him up. For a couple of weeks, he tried to continue playing. But he wasn't the same. None of the old aggressiveness. He was holding back, afraid he was going to injure someone else. Finally, he gave up and quit."

"I can understand."

"Yes," Coach Barnes said. "But it was even tougher on Chris than it might have been with some other boys. Chris was—is—an unusually sensitive boy. He feels things strongly. He felt the injury, and the repercussions, every bit as much as the boy who was hurt."

"It sounds bad."

"Yes. His parents put him in counseling, and I think it helped—helped to ease his feelings of guilt and to convince him that what happened was an

accident and that nobody was to blame." Coach
Barnes paused briefly. "But it didn't change his mind
about playing basketball. He wanted to do it, but he
just couldn't."

Coach Fulton frowned and waited for Coach
Barnes to continue.

"I spent a lot of time talking to him. So did his
father. Brian Patton thought it was important that
his son play again. He felt strongly that Chris would
regret in later years letting a freak accident end his
career. Chris really did—does—love basketball, and
something very important has been taken out of his
life."

"You say that you talked to him a lot."

"Well, I listened more than I talked. I hoped that I
was hearing him talk himself into playing again. But
it didn't happen. And, no, I was *not* going to press
him. This was something he had to decide for himself, without any shoving from me."

"I agree."

Doug thanked Coach Barnes and was about to
hang up when the Hall High coach said, "Let me
know if anything develops, or if there's anything I
can do to help. I'm interested."

"Sure. Yes, I'll let you know."

Coach Fulton hung up and leaned back in the
chair, the phone still on his lap. "Well," he said aloud
to the empty room, "so much for that crazy fantasy
coming true this year."

* * *

In the days leading up to the start of practice, Chris Patton's name came up in Coach Fulton's presence only twice.

Mary Corliss caught up with him in the corridor on the way to lunch the day after his conversation with the Hall High coach. "Did you call Indianapolis?" she asked.

Coach Fulton told her what he had learned.

"What are you going to do?"

He looked at her. "Do?" he repeated. "Nothing. Nothing at all. I'd love to see Chris Patton playing for the Panthers. From the way Coach Barnes described him, he'd probably be the difference between a fourth-place finish and the championship. But Chris is the one who's got to decide whether he plays basketball."

Mary smiled at him. "You're not a bad guy, you know."

Coach Fulton managed to grin back at her. "I'll try to remember that when we finish fourth in the conference."

Then, a week later, Bobby Hogan, a senior guard, and Hubie Willis, a senior forward, came to Coach Fulton's office after the last class of the day. He was locking his desk and preparing to leave when they appeared unexpectedly in the doorway.

"What is it?" he asked. "Come on in."

The two boys stepped inside and exchanged

glances, and then Bobby spoke. "Do you know the new boy—a transfer—named Chris Patton?"

Coach Fulton leaned back in his chair and frowned. "Have a seat," he said, waving at the two chairs against the wall.

Bobby and Hubie moved across and sat down.

"Yes, I know who he is. Why do you ask?"

Bobby continued to do the talking. "Well, he's tall, and he's got all the right moves, if you know what I mean."

Coach Fulton nodded, and fought an urge to smile. Bobby Hogan, it seemed, could spot a basketball player as well as he could.

"Well, we asked him if he'd ever played basketball."

"Uh-huh."

"And he said yeah, he had played some but didn't play anymore. That seemed funny, so I asked him why."

Coach Fulton's right eyebrow went up a notch. He was interested. "What did he say?"

Bobby gave a little shrug. "He just said he didn't like it anymore."

"That's all—just doesn't like it anymore?"

"Yes."

"And . . ."

"Nothing else, except I told him that I thought maybe he could really be a help to the team." Bobby paused. "We're kind of small, you know." He spoke as if putting the words in parentheses.

"Uh-huh," Coach Fulton said. "And what did he say?"

"He just said, 'Forget it. I don't play basketball anymore.'"

Then Hubie spoke. "We thought maybe you could talk to him."

Coach Fulton leaned forward in his chair. "I've met him, and I asked him about basketball. He told me nearly the same thing he told you—that he doesn't want to play basketball."

"But . . . ," Bobby said, and stopped. Then with a hint of anger in his eyes, he blurted, "He goes to Hamilton High. If he can help the team, he owes it to the school to play."

Coach Fulton shook his head slowly and waited a moment for Bobby to calm down. He had seen the little guard's temper flare before. It always was a brief flash that vanished as quickly as it appeared. He only hoped that Bobby wouldn't pop off at Chris Patton.

Coach Fulton selected his words carefully, figuring they were probably going to be repeated, perhaps even within earshot of Chris Patton. "If he doesn't want to play, then he doesn't want to play. We can't force him, and we don't want to even try."

On sign-up day, Coach Fulton stood in the dressing room watching the boys arrive—some of them alone, some in groups—to be weighed and measured and to receive their practice and game uniforms.

Mickey Ward, the student manager, busily went about his duties, quickly and efficiently weighing and measuring each player, marking down the figures on a chart, then handing out the uniforms.

"Gonna hit those outside ones more often this year, eh, Bobby?" he said as he handed a wire basket containing uniforms to Bobby Hogan.

Bobby grinned at Mickey, and Coach Fulton marveled again at the way the players accepted the short, chunky student manager, one of their classmates, as the mother hen of the basketball team.

Coach Fulton stood off to the side as the players

drifted in. Each time the door opened, he turned his head and looked.

Most of the players were familiar, boys returning from last year's team for their junior or senior season. To these Coach Fulton called out a word of welcome. The strangers were sophomores, up from one of Hamilton's two junior high schools, hopeful and expectant as they entered their first season with the Panthers. Doug knew some of their faces. Each season, he made it his business to attend several of the junior high games in Hamilton. He wanted to get a line on the players he had coming along. He gave each of the sophomores a smile and a nod, and pointed them toward Mickey.

But the face that Coach Fulton hoped to see coming through the door never arrived. It was a handsome one, with a wide forehead, blond hair, a narrow nose, and a strong jaw—the face of Chris Patton.

When Coach Fulton finally decided that the last player had arrived, he walked across to the table and scanned the names and figures on Mickey's chart.

"Not much height," Mickey said.

Doug glanced at Mickey with a half-smile. Sometimes the boy spoke as if he were an assistant coach, not the student manager. "Umm" was all Coach Fulton said.

Through the drills that followed, leading up to the Panthers' first game, Coach Fulton bemoaned the lack of a talented big player, capable of going up and dominating the backboards.

But there were bright spots, some of them surprising.

Hubie Willis, now a senior, clearly was ready to take a leadership role. He had held back as a sophomore and junior, deferring to the older players. But from the beginning of the drills, he led the charge on offense, and he shouted encouragement and criticism to his teammates on defense. His accuracy on baseline shots gave him added authority as a leader on the court. His development was a pleasant surprise for Coach Fulton. For any basketball team, coaching from the bench is important—but so is leadership on the court.

Alan Woodley was a sophomore, and a player Coach Fulton had looked forward to receiving. Unlike some of the other sophomores, Alan was not one of the faces Coach Fulton had trouble putting a name to. He knew Alan Woodley's name and face from watching the junior high teams. Alan was a deadly accurate shooter from the outside and a magician as a passer and dribbler. He was only about five feet seven inches tall, skinny, and looked more like a towel boy than a basketball player. But on the court he made all the right moves. He was sure to be a starter in his first year with the Panthers.

Bobby Hogan, a starter the previous season as a junior, would be Alan's partner at guard. Bobby was steady and reliable but neither quick nor clever, and he seldom offered the flash of brilliance that is the stuff of a champion. He was capable enough and dependable, but that was all.

At forward with Hubie, Coach Fulton was going to have to choose between Marty Townsend and Mark Walker, both juniors who had seen action the previous year. They were versatile but hardly more than average. Both could dribble well enough—but not brilliantly—and both could hit a fair share of their shots—but not with dazzling consistency. Both could pass—but nobody could call them unerring—and both could jump—but lacked the height and muscle to dominate. Whoever got the final nod at forward, the other was sure to be the Panthers' sixth man, the first player into the game off the bench. Both Marty and Mark could play any position in a pinch.

That left the center position, and the thought of it always put a frown on Coach Fulton's face. He conjured up the picture of Chris Patton on the court, playing as Doug was sure he could. And then the vision faded, to be replaced by reality—probably Duddy Ford.

At six feet six inches, Duddy was the tallest player on the squad. He was a senior who owned the center position after Timothy Wilson gave up early in the previous season. Duddy was expecting to play center, and Coach Fulton had to admit, he was expecting it with good reason—there was no one else. One of the sophomores was tall but gangly, lacking in both experience and confidence. He might grow, fill out a bit, and develop into a good center next year, or the next. But not this year. There was only Duddy. But the senior was slow, and a poor shooter from more than ten feet out; his hands could not always be trusted with a pass either.

At the end of the first week's final day of practice, Doug walked out of the school building with Mickey. They walked along silently, Coach Fulton's mind turning over the frustrating thought that had kept recurring all week: The Panthers were one player away from being a great team, and the one player they needed was walking the corridors of Hamilton High—Chris Patton.

Coach Fulton was heading for the parking lot, Mickey toward his house, which was less than a block away from school.

"Duddy's lousy," the student manager announced without preamble in his best assistant coach manner. "He's not even trying."

Coach Fulton, a little startled that Mickey's conclusion was so close to his own, looked at the boy's frowning face. Doug couldn't argue. Duddy was dragging himself reluctantly up and down the court, taking poor shots and missing them, passing up good shots, and loafing in the rebounding. Part of the problem, Coach Fulton knew, was that Duddy had no competition for the center position. The thought made Coach Fulton wish for the return of Timothy Wilson. Even with all his shortcomings, Timothy's presence would throw a scare into Duddy. But Coach Fulton did not say any of this to Mickey.

"Maybe Duddy will do better when the season gets under way," he said. "I've known players who couldn't hype themselves up in practice but played well in games when it really mattered."

He didn't believe this, but what else could he say to Mickey?

"Humph," Mickey said. "What about that new guy, Chris Patton?"

Coach Fulton heaved a sigh. It seemed that everyone was asking about Chris Patton playing basketball for the Hamilton High Panthers—except Chris Patton. "He's not interested in playing," Coach Fulton said.

They had reached the point where Mickey would veer off for the short walk home and Coach Fulton would continue ahead to his car in the parking lot. But Mickey stopped, and the coach stopped with him.

"He's a nice guy," Mickey said thoughtfully. "Friendly, you know."

"Chris Patton?"

"Yeah."

"You know him?"

Mickey shook his head. "No, not well. But I've got a couple of classes with him."

Coach Fulton almost smiled. "What are you getting at, Mickey?"

Mickey looked at Coach Fulton. "I could talk to him. Find out what the problem is, maybe. Straighten it out, you know." He paused, keeping his eyes on the coach. "Unless," he added, "there's a reason I shouldn't."

This time Coach Fulton not only marveled at Mickey's maturity, which was always evident, but also at the student manager's powers of perception. Indeed, there was more to the Chris Patton case than appeared on the surface. And Mickey sensed this.

But, how much to tell him?

For the time being, Doug decided, he was going to tell Mickey as little as possible. If Chris Patton wasn't talking about his problem, Coach Fulton was not going to spread the word.

He managed to smile at the boy and said, "Mickey, of course you're free to talk to him. We all are. I talked to him about coming out for basketball. Bobby and Hubie talked to him. And you can talk to him. But I did not try to pressure him when I talked to him, and I will not have you—or anyone else—trying to pressure him. Is that understood?"

Mickey grinned as if he had gotten what he wanted. "Sure," he said. "See you later."

"Right," Coach Fulton said, standing in place a moment, watching Mickey's departing back. Then he walked to his car.

At home, he called Mary Corliss. "Had dinner yet?" he asked.

"No."

"Want to go out and get something?"

"Sure."

"Only if you promise not to ask me why Chris Patton won't come out for basketball."

"Well, if that's a condition, okay."

Sometimes people dropped in to watch the Panthers practice—never a large crowd, but a couple of people on one day and maybe a half dozen on another. The businesspeople in Hamilton had to work during the afternoon, when the Panthers ran through their drills. And the students had their own activities after the last class.

Still, basketball was important in Hamilton, and an occasional fan or two showed up to watch for a few minutes. But with the Panthers' fourth-place finish in the Spoon River Conference last year and no visible evidence to indicate an improvement this year, the enthusiasm was somewhat below fever pitch in the beginning. Then, as the word began getting around about Alan Woodley's flashy ball handling and exciting shooting from the outside, more people were dropping in to take a look.

The most frequent visitor was Skip Turner, who handled the play-by-play broadcasts of the Panthers' games for the radio station. In the early days of the preseason practice, Skip often stayed until the end of practice to chat with Coach Fulton, picking up a progress report on the team for his sportscast. But Skip's main interest in watching the preseason practice sessions was to familiarize himself with the players so he could speak about them with some authority when broadcasting the games.

During the drills, Coach Fulton paid no attention to Skip or any of the other onlookers, concentrating on the work of his players on the court. But on Monday, at the height of a scrimmage, something made him glance across the court at the doorway opening into the corridor that led to the dressing room.

Chris Patton was standing there, his books held lightly in his right hand. He was watching the players weaving and screening and shooting and jumping, listening to the *thumpa-thumpa-thump* of the dribbling and the shouts of encouragement, congratulation, and criticism.

When he noticed that Coach Fulton had spotted him, he walked on.

"Did you see him watching practice?"

Mickey Ward had waited to speak until only he and the coach were left in the dressing room.

Coach Fulton looked at Mickey as he pulled on his coat. He did not need to ask who Mickey was talking about. "Yes, I saw him."

"I talked to him today."

"About basketball?"

"Uh-huh. But I didn't get anywhere. He just told me that he didn't play basketball anymore." Mickey paused and then added, "A personal thing, he said."

"Oh?"

"I wonder what he meant by that," Mickey said.

"If he says it's a personal thing, then I guess he considers it a personal thing, huh? You ready to go?"

They walked out together, down the corridor and out the basement door.

"I'll be talking to him some more," Mickey said. "I like Chris, and I think he's got a problem of some sort."

Coach Fulton glanced at the student manager in the darkness. "Don't pressure him. It's his decision."

"Sure."

As always, the date of the first game on the schedule arrived too quickly. Doug still had improvements to make. The Panthers were less than perfect, and there was a lot of polishing that remained to be done. But, no matter, the first game came up on the calendar—a home-court nonconference contest against a team from a smaller nearby high school, the New Brinkley Tigers.

The Hamilton High gymnasium was packed— every seat taken—partly because every team is a winner until the season starts, and partly, Doug was sure, because the word of Alan Woodley's spectacular play in practice had spread around town.

With noise pouring down from the bleachers on each side of the court, Coach Fulton leaned into the circle of players, grasped hands with them, and pumped three times. Then they broke and the five starters took up their positions on the court.

Doug stepped back to the bench and, still standing, watched his team. Questions raced through his mind. Had Duddy Ford believed him when he told the center: "You've goofed off through practice. First time you goof off in this game, you're coming out"? Had Duddy believed him? Who knew? Was Alan Woodley nervous about this, his first varsity game for Hamilton High? Coach Fulton had told him: "This is just like practice, only more fun." Did Alan believe him? There was no way to tell what the slight guard with the deadpan face was thinking.

But in the first five minutes of play, Coach Fulton got some of his answers.

Duddy Ford was working hard. He ran with all he had. He tried hard for rebounds. He concentrated on his shots, taking more good ones and passing up more bad ones than he had done in practice. But he remained slow and unsure.

As for Alan Woodley, he dribbled around and past defenders as if he owned them, and he hit the net for three field goals in the opening minutes, leading the Panthers to a quick 12–4 margin. So much for worrying about Alan's nervousness.

With Bobby Hogan unselfishly feeding the ball to

Alan, and Hubie Willis getting hot from the baseline, the Panthers finished the first half with a 32–19 lead over the New Brinkley Tigers.

Leaving the bench for the trek to the dressing room for halftime, Coach Fulton walked behind his players, gazing at nothing. He hardly heard the roaring cheer of the Hamilton High fans. But as he turned at the end of the court, he saw Chris Patton standing at the edge of the bleachers, watching the Panthers walk toward the dressing room.

When the team returned to the court for the start of the second half, Doug consciously looked around for Chris. He did not see him. Nor did he spot him in those moments during the play in the second half when he caught himself glancing around.

On the court, the Panthers continued their romp, finishing with a 63–41 victory, led by Alan Woodley's twenty-three points.

The players whooped and hollered and cheered in the dressing room. They had won their first game, and by a runaway score. But Coach Fulton knew that the New Brinkley Tigers were a weak team, a suitable season opener, a mild test. And, as such, potentially dangerous for the Panthers' future.

The Panthers lost their next game, a 51–50 heartbreaker, to the Castleton High Ramblers when Duddy Ford, all alone under the basket, muffed a pass with six seconds remaining on the clock. The ball slithered off his fingertips and bounced out of bounds, turning possession over to the Ramblers, who succeeded in running out the clock. That was Monday night.

They bounced back with a 57–51 triumph over the Burlington High Eagles on Thursday night, but Coach Fulton walked off the court at the end of the game feeling like anything but a winner. The Eagles, while losing, had outplayed the Panthers.

On Friday, with the sour taste of the unimpressive victory over Burlington High still bothering him, he kept the players in the dressing room after they had changed for practice.

"This week," he said, "we lost a game we should have won, and we won a game we should have lost. In both cases, it was a pretty sad showing."

He looked around at the faces turned toward him. None of them showed any surprise at his opening remark. They probably knew the facts as well as he.

"We are a better team than the Castleton High Ramblers, and we should have beaten them. I'm not talking about any last-second shot being missed. I'm talking about the whole game. The Ramblers shouldn't have even been close to us at the finish, much less in the lead."

He paused and wondered about the wisdom of letting Duddy off the hook so easily. Duddy could have won the game for the Panthers. By concentrating he could have caught the pass. And by concentrating he could have made the game-winning field goal. But Coach Fulton's iron rule forbade public criticism. There was nothing to be gained in humiliating a player in front of his teammates. Besides, the whole team had seen Duddy fumble the pass, and Duddy surely knew he had fumbled the pass. That was enough, the coach figured.

"And against Burlington High," he continued, "you let the Eagles beat you at everything but the score. Chalk that one up to luck. We won, but I felt like a loser. The Eagles played tougher defense, fought harder on the boards, and concentrated all

32

the way. I don't know how we won. Like I said, luck, I guess."

Surely he thought, everyone in the room knew that Alan Woodley's deadeye shooting was what bailed them out.

"Luck," he repeated. Then he added, "And Alan's shooting. Well, you can't bumble your way through a game, just hoping that Alan will hit another shot."

He looked at the serious faces around him. Not one of these boys had ever played on a winning team—a real winner. Not one of them had felt the thrill of being a champion. They didn't know what they were missing. How could Coach Fulton explain it to them?

He took a breath. "Today, when we take the court for practice, we are beginning the season again. Our first beginning was not good, so we'll try again. This time, we'll all concentrate. We will never—never—rest on defense. We will work very hard. Okay?"

Some of the somber faces nodded at him.

"And," Coach Fulton concluded, "those who don't work very, very hard are going to be watching the games from the bench."

After the warm-up shots, Doug divided the squad and sent them into a full-speed scrimmage.

Alan Woodley darted around the court with dazzling brilliance. He hit the basket time and again from the outside. He wriggled through crowds of defenders to score on lay-ups. On defense, he pestered his opponents to distraction.

Duddy Ford tried hard. Coach Fulton had to give him that. But even with his best effort, Duddy was limited in what he could accomplish. Big enough to be a factor on the boards, he lacked the coordination to put himself in the right spot in the right position at the right moment. And he lacked that one intangible that all the great players displayed—a fierce competitiveness in going after the ball.

Hubie Willis, Bobby Hogan, and the others all worked hard too, with Hubie urging everyone on to greater effort.

Despite his concentration on each move of every player, Coach Fulton caught himself more than once glancing at the doorway at the end of the gym. Maybe, he thought, Chris Patton will be standing there, watching. But the doorway was always empty.

Finally, fifteen minutes later than the usual quitting time, Coach Fulton called an end to the drill.

"That was better, much better," he told the puffing and sweat-streaked players.

Then he sent them to the showers.

As for Doug Fulton, he went to his apartment and headed into a weekend of housekeeping chores, and a weekend of brooding about his basketball team.

The young season—now only three games old—already was resembling the past ones. The Panthers were a team with some strengths, capable of winning some games. But they had weaknesses that were going to cost them a lot of victories. He could not escape the feeling that his team was doomed to fourth place in the Spoon River Conference again.

Chris Patton's face kept invading Coach Fulton's thoughts and, time and again, he shook his head in an effort to make the image go away.

He had not seen Chris at either of the last two games. Nor had he spotted him again sneaking a glimpse of the Panthers' practice session. But he did, of course, see Chris occasionally in the corridors. The tall boy with the broad shoulders always nodded a greeting, sometimes said, "Good morning, Coach," but that was all. Coach Fulton always nodded back.

On Sunday, Mary called. "If you don't have anything else going, come on over this evening for dinner."

Doug actually smiled into the telephone. Her invitation came as a welcome relief. He was weary of wrestling with basketball questions that didn't seem to have any answers.

"You're on," he said. "What time?"

Doug steered his Volkswagen through the long shadows of the early evening, heading for Mary's apartment. She lived in a long low row of apartments facing Barton Elementary School, across town from Coach Fulton's apartment near Hamilton High.

He turned the last corner, to go around the school's playground, and headed for the apartment building.

To his left, the playground was empty in the deepening shadows except for—what?

Coach Fulton was already past the basketball backboard on the playground before his eye told his brain that a solitary boy was shooting free throws, and that the boy looked like Chris Patton.

He slowed his car and turned his head, looking back just in time to see the ball drop through the hoop and the boy—yes, he did look like Chris Patton—jog forward to retrieve it. The boy took in the ball, dribbled once, and laid it back up on the rim.

Coach Fulton drove to the corner, turned left, and kept going past Mary's apartment. Two more lefts and he had circled the block. Coming up behind the lone figure shooting baskets, he slowed again, and watched.

No question, the shooter was Chris.

Doug drove on past, took the left at the corner again, and pulled to the curb in front of Mary's apartment.

"Was that you I saw driving past just a moment ago?" Mary asked when she opened the door.

Doug laughed and said, "Yes, it was."

"You seem awfully happy about it. I thought maybe you had just remembered a better offer."

Doug walked across to the front window, bent,

and peered out. Then he straightened back up. "You can't see him from here," he said.

"See who? Are you sure you're all right?"

"Chris Patton is shooting baskets on the playground."

"So . . . ?"

Doug shrugged and smiled at Mary. "It's progress," he said. "What's for dinner?"

On Monday, the Panthers rode the school bus the twenty-five miles to William Joyce High School, in the town of Webster. The Joyce High Pioneers, undefeated in three games, were the Panthers' final non-conference opponent before moving into the Spoon River Conference race for the championship.

Coach Fulton knew that his "new beginning" was in for a tough test. A smaller school, Joyce High clearly had a good team. They had won their first three games and would not give up the undefeated label easily. Their coach, a veteran approaching retirement, was a crafty tactician with an almost mystical ability to get the most out of his players. The Pioneers also had the advantage of the home court: their own fans shrieking for victory, their own families and friends watching. Doug figured the home-court advantage was worth five to ten points in any basketball game.

From the opening tip, he thought the Panthers were going to win. Even Duddy Ford's face wore an expression of intensity. Alan Woodley stole the ball out of a Joyce High player's hands before the game was thirty seconds old, zipped a pass to Hubie in the corner, and the senior forward lofted the ball into the net. Best of all, in Doug's mind, was the fact that Duddy was there for the rebound in case the shot missed.

By halftime, the Panthers were leading 31–27.

Following his players to the dressing room for the break, Coach Fulton let his thoughts trail back over the action in the first half, and he was reminded again that Duddy—even Duddy trying hard—lacked the ability and the innate competitiveness of a real winner. The Panthers, while leading, were a team with a hole at the center position.

In the dressing room, the coach nodded approval and told his team, "You're playing well. But, remember, we have a second half left to play." Then he made a couple of adjustments in the defense and offered the obvious advice, "Get the ball to Alan on the outside and Hubie in the corner, whenever you can."

The Pioneers came out for the second half like a team possessed. With their two big players, the center and a forward, locking up the backboards and their guards grabbing the ball at every turn, they went on a nine-point run, taking the lead at 36–31 before Coach Fulton called a time-out.

While his players were approaching him at the bench, he turned involuntarily and glanced down the court at the opposition bench. The gray-haired, slightly stooped coach of the Joyce High Pioneers was waiting for his own players. Doug wondered what the veteran coach had told his team in the dressing room to set off a nine-point run.

"Take it easy and just breathe for a minute," Coach Fulton told the players. "They got hot, and now we've got to cool them off." He replaced Marty Townsend at forward with the slightly taller Mark Walker and told Mark to join Duddy under the boards. "We've got to stop those two tall guys. Block 'em out."

With Alan Woodley hot from the outside, the Panthers finished on top—but only barely, 58–54. Alan finished with twenty-two points.

As for Coach Fulton, he was thankful to escape with a victory, and he heaved a sigh of relief when the bus pulled away from the Joyce High gymnasium.

Next morning, Doug ran through the rain from his car to the basement door of Hamilton High. Inside, he took off his raincoat and shook the water off it. Then he walked down the corridor toward his office, pulling his key out of his pocket as he went.

Chris Patton was standing in front of his office door, waiting.

Chris said nothing, but stepped away from the door.

Doug nodded to him, inserted the key in the lock, turned it, and opened the door. "Come on in," he said.

Chris followed Coach Fulton into the small office. Doug closed the door and gestured to the wooden chair alongside his desk. Doug walked around his desk and took a seat.

The boy looks like a basketball player even just sitting there, Doug thought.

Aloud he said, "Well, Chris."

"Coach, I'd like to come out for the basketball team," he said softly. He was not grinning in obvious anticipation of the coach's grateful acceptance, and that was good. And he was not scowling with the intensity of a boy who takes himself too seriously. He had simply stated his intention. Then, with a slight movement of his head, he added, "If it's not too late."

Coach Fulton watched him, and some unexpected thoughts began racing through his mind. Sure, he had felt his heart skip a beat when he saw Chris Patton standing outside his office door. Why not? Probably Chris was what the Hamilton High Panthers needed to contend for the Spoon River Conference championship. Without him, they undoubtedly were destined to win a few, lose a few, and wallow around in the middle of the standings. Naturally, he was excited at the prospect of adding this player of proven ability to the lineup.

But now Doug wondered: Has Chris Patton overcome the terrible effects of having seriously injured a boy in a game? Has he thought through this decision? Is he really sure this is what he wants to do? Or was it a flip decision, a spur-of-the-moment action? Has he discussed this decision with his parents? What do they think? The questions whirled around in Coach Fulton's mind.

Chris Patton offered him no help with the answers. He did not relate the story of the tragic accident. He did not mention his reasons for rejecting Coach Fulton's overture in the preseason. He said nothing. He just waited.

"Of course it's not too late," Doug said. "We'll be happy to have you."

As he watched Chris, he wanted to ask if he'd told his parents of his decision. What if they had changed their minds about wanting their son to play basketball? Then he shrugged off the thought. Either way, they would have the final say; a parent had to sign a waiver of responsibility before a student could participate in a varsity sport.

"Today?" Chris asked. "Can I start today?"

Instead of pleasing Doug, Chris's pressing for an immediate start served to add more questions to those already circling through his mind. Did Chris, maybe with lingering uncertainty about his decision, want to start right away before he had a chance to change his mind? Or was he acting without his parents' knowledge and wanting to present them with an accomplished fact? Or was he, perhaps, simply eager to get going?

Coach Fulton said, "There's the matter of the waiver of responsibility signed by a parent. It's required of all students coming out for varsity sports."

Chris nodded. "I know. My father's expecting it. His office is in the Gould Building. If there's some way . . ."

Coach Fulton smiled. With hardly more than a dozen words, Chris had answered some of the questions. "All right, we'll get it to him somehow," he said. "Sure, start today."

Chris stood up and said, "Okay." Then he stood there a second, seeming to have something more to say. Finally, he said it. "I've played basketball before."

Coach Fulton grinned up at him. This was no time to get into a discussion of his telephone conversation with Coach Barnes and all the background it involved. "I was sure you had, the first time I saw you" was all that Doug said.

Chris left, and seconds later the bell rang for the first class, summoning not only the students but also the coach to his first-period gym class.

But Doug sat at his desk for a moment, not moving. He picked up a pencil and absently played with it. If the boy was good—and his former coach in Indianapolis said he was more than just good—this should be a cause for celebration. But Coach Fulton was frowning. He wondered what had brought Chris Patton around from saying, "I'm not a basketball player," to saying, "I'd like to come out for the team." Would he be able to play the backboards, scramble for the ball, without seeing a boy holding a hand to an injured eye?

Doug put down the pencil, shoved back the desk chair, and bent over, switching from loafers to sneakers, and then walked around to the dressing room, where the boys were changing for gym class.

At nine forty-five, the beginning of his open period, Coach Fulton walked to the school office to pick up a waiver form and take another look into the file of Chris Patton. He needed Chris's father's office phone number.

"What changed his mind?" Mary Corliss asked.

She and Doug were standing behind the front counter in the school office.

"I don't know. He didn't say anything except that he wanted to come out for the team. And he told me he had played basketball before. That was all."

"You didn't tell him you had spoken to Coach Barnes, and that you knew . . . ?"

"Nope. He didn't mention the accident, and I let it go at that. I think it's best to play it his way, at least for now."

Doug turned to go but stopped when he heard his name called. He looked around and found the student clerk at the switchboard gesturing to him. "You have a phone call," she said. "Do you want to take it here or in your office?"

Mary said, "You can use my desk."

He nodded and walked across to the desk. When the telephone rang, he picked it up. "Hello."

"Coach Fulton?"

"Yes, speaking."

"My name is Brian Patton. I'm Chris Patton's father."

"I was just about to give you a call—to ask if I could drop by with his waiver for you to sign." Then he added, "And to meet you."

"Then my son has spoken with you?"

"Yes. This morning. Before the first class."

After a pause, Mr. Patton said, "Coach Fulton, there is an unusual circumstance involved in Chris's case. Did he mention this to you?"

"No, he didn't. But I'm aware of the background. I spoke with Coach Barnes in Indianapolis."

"You did?"

"Yes. I was interested in Chris and curious about his lack of interest in basketball."

"I see."

Another pause followed.

"I think that you and I need to talk," Brian Patton said.

"I agree. I'd like that."

A secretary ushered Doug through an outer office into Brian Patton's office—a large room, carpeted and furnished with heavy padded chairs, with one wall of solid glass looking out over downtown Hamilton.

The man who came around the desk to greet Coach Fulton looked as if he might have been a basketball player himself in his day. He was tall, muscular, and rangy, and he carried himself like an athlete.

"It's Doug, isn't it?" he said in a friendly way, extending his hand.

"Yes. Doug." The coach shook Mr. Patton's hand.

"I'm Brian. Have a seat. I appreciate this. I know you're a busy man during the season."

Coach Fulton sat in a comfortably padded chair, and Brian Patton returned around the desk to his chair.

Coach Fulton waited.

"You know what happened?"

"Yes."

"After a lot of soul-searching, his mother and I decided that the best thing for Chris was to return to basketball, play the game that he loves, and convince himself that what happened was a once-in-a-lifetime accident and not his fault. Even the injured boy's parents kept insisting it was an accident—no one's fault. They seemed to feel as sorry for Chris in his dilemma as they felt for their own son. Lucy— Chris's mother—and I told him our feelings on the matter. But we also told him that the final decision was his. You know what that decision was until very recently."

"Yes."

"When I called you, I wanted you to know the background. When I learned that you already knew, I wanted to meet you and tell you that his mother and I support his playing basketball, but only if he is really able to overcome the memory of the accident."

"I understand."

"If the fear—and that's what it is, fear—over- takes him, he's got to quit. I mean, instantly. We don't want to damage our son. What we want is for him to recover."

Coach Fulton nodded and thought he saw what was coming next.

"As his coach, you're the one who will see first if the specter of that accident is tearing him apart.

You'll be the one with him—on road games, for example—and the first one to see good signs or, heaven forbid, bad signs. And we will be counting on you to take the necessary action and to do so promptly."

"Of course."

Brian Patton leaned back and smiled suddenly. "Doug, are you still sure you want my boy on your team?"

Coach Fulton walked into the dressing room a few minutes late. He looked around. Mickey Ward was gathering up towels and picking up a couple of basketballs to take to the court. Bobby Hogan was half dressed for practice. Hubie Willis was undressing. Duddy Ford was walking in the door. Chris Patton was not in sight.

Doug walked across to Mickey. "Lay out another uniform," he said. "We may be gaining a new player today."

Mickey looked up at the coach. Surprise flickered across his face, but lasted only a second. Then he said, "Chris Patton?"

Mickey Ward is a very bright boy, Coach Fulton thought. But all he said was, "I think so."

"All *right!*"

Then Chris entered.

"Come in, Chris," Coach Fulton said. "Over here, for your measurements and uniforms."

"Sure," Chris said. He spoke the word softly and kept his eye on Coach Fulton, then turned to look at Mickey.

To Coach Fulton he seemed to be unsure of himself, perhaps a little nervous. Maybe he was having second thoughts. Maybe he was forcing himself to do something that, in truth, frightened him.

Heads turned all around the dressing room, but no one said anything. The room was deathly quiet. Bobby Hogan's eyebrows went up, and Coach Fulton noticed that he glanced at Duddy. Hubie grinned openly. Duddy frowned. Anyone of Chris Patton's size was sure to be a candidate for the center position.

Coach Fulton heard Alan Woodley's whispered voice in the silence: "Who is he?"

Nobody answered.

For the benefit of Alan and anyone else who did not already know Chris from a classroom or corridor chatter, Coach Fulton said, "This is Chris Patton, a transfer student from Indianapolis. He's joining the team today."

Chris, seeming a little embarrassed, gave a blank-faced nod to the group.

Coach Fulton said to him, "Get your stuff from Mickey."

Mickey, weighing Chris and measuring him, marked down the figures and handed a basket containing uniforms and a towel to him, saying, "Here we go."

Coach Fulton called out, "Let's go! Let's go! The Leesville Bears are coming up Thursday night for the start of the conference season. We've got a lot of work to do."

Coach Fulton stood at the sideline in front of the empty bleachers, hands on hips, and watched Chris Patton taking warm-up shots. Chris was big, standing six feet seven inches according to Mickey's measurements. He was broad-shouldered, slender but muscular.

He was taking his shots from just beyond the free-throw line, a little to the left—sending them off and then jogging easily to the basket to retrieve the ball.

He delivered his shots with a feather touch seldom seen in such a large boy. Doug Fulton remembered only one other player with such a light touch, a teammate in college. He himself had never mastered the art of such ease in sending the ball on its way to the basket.

Chris sank three in a row before he missed, and Coach Fulton, glancing around, realized that all his players were watching the new boy on the team. If Chris was aware he was performing for an audience, he did not show it.

The coach clapped his hands together loudly three times and called out, "Okay, okay, let's run some patterns." He turned to Chris. "Patton, you at center. You've got a lot to learn, and now is the time to start."

For forty minutes they weaved through plays, dribbled, screened, shot, rebounded—a controlled drill aimed primarily at teaching Chris the way that Coach Fulton wanted a basketball game to be played.

Then he called five boys over from their work at the other end of the court and put in a defense against a first five built around Chris.

Coach Fulton called a play, then backed off the court, beyond the sideline stripe. He took a couple more long steps and sat down on the front bleacher seat, elbow on his knee, chin resting on his fist, and watched.

This was it. This was the test. So Chris Patton could pump in shots with a rare beauty of movement from the edge of the keyhole. So he could quickly grasp the intricacies of the plays used by the Hamilton High Panthers. So he could dribble better than most big players and was sure-handed in taking a pass. But all of that was without an opponent in his face, stabbing and grabbing at the ball, bumping him—and reminding him of a tragic accident.

Could Chris Patton fight his way to the boards for a rebound? Could he scramble for a loose ball on the court?

Coach Fulton was about to get the answers to those questions. And so, too, he figured, was Chris Patton.

As the play got under way on the court, Chris's face gave no clue to his thoughts. His eyes were alert, following the ball. If there were dark thoughts of a terrible accident in his mind, they surely were buried deep at this moment. He was concentrating on the play unfolding around him. He moved quickly and confidently, a boy playing a game he had mastered.

The play that Coach Fulton had directed the offense to run had the ball winding up in Hubie's hands near the sideline. If he was open, Hubie would take a long shot. Chris would be out in front of the basket—maybe to take a pass for a lay-up, maybe to go up for a rebound if Hubie's shot missed.

Coach Fulton waited, watching the players weave through their pattern, passing and handing off.

Then Hubie had the ball. He was open for a second and shot for the basket.

Chris turned, watching the arc of the shot, and moved back toward a position under the basket. Duddy, guarding him, went with him.

Hubie's shot was off the mark by a fraction of an

inch. The ball hit the rim and seemed to rest there, as if trying to decide whether to fall through or off to the side. Then it bounded out and up a little and began coming down.

Chris was off the floor, hands high. Duddy was with him.

Chris twisted—it had to be instinctive—and put his body between the path of the ball and Duddy. Duddy was cut off, helpless to do anything.

Chris's rising hands grasped the falling ball, and he dropped back to the court, flat-footed, holding the ball with both hands. He fired a pass out to Alan Woodley.

Coach Fulton took a deep breath. He felt he really needed it. Chris Patton had done it, and apparently with no doubts, no hesitation. But Doug knew he had seen the move that caused the accident. Chris's instinctive motion to cut off his opponent could send an elbow crashing into an opponent's head.

The coach shouted out the next play to the players on the court.

After practice, while the players were showering, Coach Fulton stepped out of the dressing room and around the corner to his office. He closed the door, sat at his desk, looked up a number in a telephone directory, and dialed.

"Brian?"

"Yes."

"Doug Fulton."

"Yes?" The question mark gave Brian Patton's voice a shade of apprehension.

"It went beautifully. I knew you must be wondering. If Chris had the first thought about the accident—if he had the first doubt about playing—it didn't show. He was aggressive and, I might add, very, very able."

"That's good news."

"On the court," Coach Fulton said, "Chris was like a boy who had come home at last."

Brian Patton chuckled. "That's great. I appreciate the call, Doug."

Coach Fulton replaced the receiver and sat a moment, his hand still on the telephone. He owed one more telephone report—to Coach Barnes in Indianapolis. He glanced at his watch: five thirty-five. Probably Coach Barnes was winding down his own practice session at Hall High. Better to call him this evening from home.

Doug got up and returned to the dressing room.

Throughout practice the next day, Wednesday, with Chris dominating with every step he took, Duddy Ford seemed to actually shrink in size. Chris and Duddy both were centers, and natural opponents in scrimmage. Chris was only an inch taller than Duddy, but he seemed more. Duddy, quickly deciding he was sure to be whipped—whether trying to guard Chris or trying to get a shot past him—was surrendering more and more frequently before the battle was fought.

Duddy had lost his starting center role, and he, and everyone else, knew it without having to be told.

Maybe, Coach Fulton thought, the sudden and unexpected appearance of a new player so clearly Duddy's superior in talent had hit him like a shock wave. Maybe Duddy would adjust to the new fact of life and play his best, given time.

But when Duddy seemed to withdraw even more in the Wednesday practice—giving up, even blushing with embarrassment on a couple of occasions—Coach Fulton hailed him as he was leaving the dressing room to head for home.

"A minute," Coach Fulton said, joining him at the door. "Let's go around here." Without waiting for a reply, he led Duddy into the corridor and around the corner, to his office.

Standing in Coach Fulton's office, Duddy looked embarrassed. He's sure I'm going to tell him that he's lost his starter position, Coach Fulton thought. Well, I am.

"Sit down, please."

Duddy took a seat and Coach Fulton walked around his desk and sat down.

"I think I'm going to quit," Duddy said without preamble.

"Don't."

"You—the team—you don't need me anymore. You've always said that I don't try hard enough. Well, you've got somebody now who does."

Coach Fulton studied Duddy's forlorn face for a moment. He and the team did need Duddy—because Chris Patton might last no longer than the first collision under the basket in a hard-fought game. Chris had passed the test in practice, but a game was something else. However, the needs of the coach and the team were secondary right now to the needs of Duddy Ford.

Coach Fulton leaned across the desk toward Duddy. "First of all, saying that the team doesn't need you is like saying the team doesn't need Mark Walker, who spends a lot of time on the bench watching Marty Townsend play forward. Mark is every bit as much a part of this team as Marty. And you will be every bit as much a part of the team as Chris, even if Chris is starting at center. No basketball team is just five players. We're a team, a squad."

Duddy was looking at the floor now, and he didn't appear to be at all convinced.

"I think you'd be making a mistake you would regret if you quit, Duddy. You've been a part of the team for three years. This is your senior year. You belong out there with the team, not sitting in the bleachers, watching and wishing you were down there with your teammates."

Duddy nodded slightly. "I'll think about it."

* * *

The noise from the pep band and the crowd jammed into the gymnasium for the Panthers' game with the Leesville Bears—the opening game of the race for the Spoon River Conference championship—filled the dressing room.

Beyond the fans' natural inclination to attend their team's games, the word of Alan Woodley's spectacular outside shooting had stirred excitement. Little Alan Woodley, a sophomore, was the talk of Hamilton.

Undoubtedly word about Chris Patton had gotten around town too. First, as just a new player joining the team late, and then after the first practice, as a potentially great player. Players told their families and friends, and they told other people. News traveled that way in Hamilton. But nobody outside the team had seen Chris play even in practice, much less in a game.

Coach Fulton, seated on the training table, had watched the players enter, go to their lockers, and dress for the game.

To the coach's relief, Duddy Ford was one of the first to appear. He nodded to Coach Fulton and moved on past. The coach said simply, "Duddy," as if they had not had their conversation the previous evening.

When Chris Patton entered, Coach Fulton looked at him closely. Practice was one thing, and Chris certainly had passed the test, but a game was something else again. The boy nodded and smiled at

Coach Fulton when their eyes met. If Chris Patton was nervous about his first game since the accident—and also his first game before a crowd in his new hometown—he was doing a good job of hiding the fact. He walked across to his locker and began undressing.

The others came in: Hubie, Bobby, Alan, all of them.

When they all had changed into their game uniforms—green trimmed with gold—Coach Fulton slid off the training table and stood in front of them.

"We'll start Townsend and Willis at forwards, Patton at center, and Woodley and Hogan at guards," he said as matter-of-factly as he could. He avoided looking at Duddy.

"The Bears have lost two of their four games. They ought to be duck soup for us. But if you think so, we're in deep trouble. This is the Spoon River Conference race now, and it means more. They'll be trying harder; and if you're not trying harder, we can find ourselves getting whipped. Any team—any team at all—can run over a team that's lax. So let's concentrate, work hard, and win."

He glanced around at the faces. Most of them were somber. Bobby Hogan was grinning, eager to get into the action. Chris Patton's face was blank.

"All right, let's go," Doug said.

The players got up and streamed through the door, their coach following them.

* * *

As he delivered his lineup to the official at the scorer's table between the benches, something caused Coach Fulton to look up, toward the top row of bleacher seats, and then beyond. There, at the little table on the platform that passed for a broadcasting booth in the Hamilton High gym, Skip Turner was having what might be called a barely controlled fit. Although he continued to talk into his microphone, he was waving his arms and his face was contorted into an expression of anger.

Coach Fulton slammed the palm of his right hand onto his forehead.

Obviously, the broadcaster had noticed the tall and muscular stranger wearing the green and gold uniform, now sinking a gently flicked shot. Who was the new player? Skip Turner had not dropped by practice on Tuesday or Wednesday. Clearly, none of the talk about Chris had reached him. And Coach Fulton had not thought to call him. Now Skip was on the air, needing to explain something he knew nothing about.

Coach Fulton gave a nod and a little wave of his right hand and then hurried back to the bench, seeking Mickey Ward.

"Mickey, climb up there and tell Skip Turner that Chris Patton is a transfer student who just joined the team—and hurry, or Skip will kill me."

CHAPTER

7

Chris won the opening tip, flicked the ball to Alan Woodley to his left, and ran for the basket. Alan dribbled the ball a couple of steps and fired it inside to Chris. Chris took in the pass, dribbled once, turned and went up, and, with his beautiful light touch, laid the ball into the basket.

The packed gymnasium erupted in a roar. To the few who had heard about Chris Patton, the first look at him in action backed up the story. But for most of the fans in the bleachers, the player at center was a stranger, and a murmuring of questions—who is he?—lingered after the cheering had died out.

Chris's play—so authoritative, so perfect—was, Coach Fulton had to concede from his seat on the bench, a bit awesome. Coach Fulton remained seated, unmoving and blank-faced, as the Leesville Bears brought the ball inbounds for their first possession. But behind the blank expression, Coach Fulton felt a sense of excitement. For a brief moment, he enjoyed replaying in his mind the movements of Chris Patton turning, going up, and almost lovingly placing the ball in the basket. Every movement was perfect. He had physical coordination that was rare in a boy so large.

On the court, Bobby Hogan promptly stole the ball from a Leesville guard in mid-dribble, turned and eluded the guard's frustrated jab at recovering the ball, and fired a pass across to Alan Woodley. Alan dribbled forward, stopped, and shot—*swoosh!*

The game was barely seconds old and Hamilton High led 4–0. The Leesville Bears had not yet succeeded in getting the ball across the center stripe. Coach Fulton stared at the ceiling of the gymnasium as the Leesville guard flipped the ball inbounds again.

The Bears crossed the center stripe this time, and a pass put the ball into the hands of a player in the corner. He took a step forward and shot. But he was one second too late. With two large steps, Chris landed in front of him and, leaping, blocked the shot with his outstretched right hand. The ball fell into Hubie Willis's hands. Hubie turned and passed to Marty Townsend, racing down the court. Marty brought in the ball, dribbled twice, and laid it up. It circled the rim and fell off. Chris, coming behind Marty, grabbed the ball.

Chris passed the ball to Alan, then drifted out from under the basket.

Alan sent the ball back to Chris, and Chris, near the free throw line, sent a softly sailing push shot into the net.

The scoreboards on the wall at each end of the gymnasium blinked to 6–0.

The Leesville coach called a time-out.

Coach Fulton was grateful for the time-out. He had the frightening feeling that his team was using up a whole season's worth of good fortune in the first couple of minutes of a game against a team that was already twice beaten. His Panthers were going to need some of that luck against tougher teams on the schedule.

The players gathered around him at the sideline. Bobby Hogan was grinning, obviously enjoying himself. Chris was watching Coach Fulton, waiting for him to speak.

With the time-out, the pep band swung into noisy action, and the crowd was cheering and clapping in time to the music. The combination was deafening.

"You've really stunned them," Coach Fulton said, leaning into the circle of players and almost shouting to be heard above the din. "Now, keep the pressure on. They're down there trying to regroup, hoping a time-out will cool you off. Play your own game, and be alert." He looked at Alan and said, "Put it up there." Alan nodded his head jerkily. Coach Fulton then turned to Chris and, with half a smile, said, "If Alan misses, you grab it." Chris said simply, "Okay," as if the instruction were insightful and the execution automatic.

By halftime, the Panthers were leading, 45–27. Duddy Ford was in the game at center, and Mark Walker had replaced Marty Townsend at forward.

"Keep doing what you're doing," Coach Fulton told the players in the dressing room. "I know that I'm supposed to frighten you with a story about a team that led by eighteen points at the halftime and then got defeated by a great comeback. But that's not going to happen to you tonight—if you keep going the way you're going."

The players were scattered on benches in front of him. Chris, who scored fourteen points before retiring in favor of Duddy, and Alan, who had sixteen points, were seated together. Duddy, whose few minutes on the court were the best he had had in the young season, was dripping with sweat. He had worked hard and would start the second half.

"Don't get careless, don't loosen up, don't give them anything," Coach Fulton said, and sent them back to the court.

The score at the finish was 71–57, with everyone on the Hamilton High bench getting playing time.

The dressing room was filled with laughter and whoops and cheers. Bobby Hogan even did a mock dribble and shot for the imaginary goal—a play that ended with a wet towel hitting him in the face. He was laughing when he pulled the towel away. Chris was grinning and nodding and accepting congratulations from his teammates. Even Duddy was grinning as he acknowledged bits of praise for his play. Probably now, Coach Fulton thought, Duddy is pleased with his decision to stay with the team. Only Alan Woodley, the sophomore sharpshooter who finished as the game's high scorer with twenty-four points, looked reserved, cautious, even unsure. Still feeling something of an outsider, he watched the juniors and seniors with wonder written all over his face. It's okay, Coach Fulton told himself. Alan will discover shortly that he is a member of the team.

Doug held his hands in the air and called out above the din: "Hear this! Hear this!"

Gradually, the noise of the winning dressing room faded away.

"You played a great game, and you won it easily," he said, and somebody—probably Bobby Hogan—shouted, "Yeah!"

"But remember two things," the coach went on. "One, the Leesville Bears are not the best team we will face in the Spoon River Conference this year. And two, we're going to practice tomorrow like we lost the game."

Somebody—again, probably Bobby Hogan—emitted a long groaning, "Oooooh."

"Now into the showers. We don't want anyone coming down with a cold."

When the last of the players had showered, dressed, and walked out of the dressing room, Coach Fulton pulled on his coat and looked around for Mickey Ward. The student manager was gathering up the last few towels left on the benches.

"Lock 'er up when you leave, will you, Mickey?"

"Sure." Then, with only the two of them in the dressing room, Mickey said, "We've got a winner, haven't we?"

Coach Fulton grinned. "Maybe," he said. "I'll be able to tell you for sure when the season is over."

Stepping from the dressing room into the corridor, Doug wasn't surprised to find himself facing George Holman, the editor of the *Hamilton Weekly Post,* and Skip Turner. Coach Fulton grinned sheepishly.

George Holman was frowning the frown of a newspaper editor who knew he had missed a story. The *Hamilton Weekly Post,* published each Thursday, had come out this very day without a word about a new player—a spectacular player, at that—joining the Panthers.

Skip Turner, wearing an expression of outrage, spoke first. "Doug, where did that boy come from? Where have you been hiding him? Why weren't we told?" He fired out the words like rifle shots. Skip wasn't asking questions, he was demanding answers. Clearly, he had been caught flat-footed on the air, needing to explain the new name in the lineup who was pouring points through the basket—and having no real explanation to offer. Thanks to Mickey's arrival, he was able to say that Chris Patton was a transfer student. But where, his listeners might wonder, did he come from? And why, they might wonder, was he joining the team at this late date? Skip had been forced to leave his listeners wondering.

Coach Fulton looked from Skip to George and then back to Skip. He had had little experience with the news media. When he was a player in college, his coach simply did not allow media access to members of the team. And as coach at Hamilton High, he dealt with Holman and Turner in preseason appraisals of the team and took the occasional question about somebody's physical fitness during the season. Skip sometimes dropped by to watch practice—but, as luck would have it, not this week. Holman never appeared at practice. So, if the truth be known, it had never occurred to Doug in the past two very busy days to fill in either newsman. He should have done it, but he never thought of it. Would Holman and Turner believe that?

"I'm sorry," he said finally. "Chris Patton only decided to come out for the team a couple of days ago. There were a lot of things to do. My mind was on other things. I just didn't think to call you."

Nobody spoke for a minute.

Then Skip Turner said, "He's a transfer? From where?"

"Indianapolis," Coach Fulton said slowly, not liking the idea of Skip Turner pursuing Chris's background.

Holman said, "He wasn't on the preseason list you gave us for publication."

Mickey Ward emerged from the dressing room, gave a quizzical glance to the three of them standing in the corridor, then locked the door and walked past them, saying, "Good night."

As Coach Fulton watched the student manager disappear around the corner, he made a decision. Swearing Holman and Turner to secrecy, he would tell them Chris Patton's story. Better that, he figured, than to have one of them call Coach Barnes and then reveal Chris's secret to the world.

"Look," he said, taking a deep breath, "we can't talk standing around here. I'll meet you at Rudley's and we can have a cup of coffee while I explain what's happened."

George Holman and Skip Turner gave little nods.

Led by Chris Patton's sure domination of the backboards, his feather-touch shooting, and his gentle tips-ins—plus the outside accuracy of quiet sophomore guard Alan Woodley—the Panthers rolled over every team in their path during the next two weeks. With their latest victory, a 65–48 thrashing of Bunford High, they stood alone at the top of the Spoon River Conference standings. They were 5–0 in conference games, the only undefeated team.

Through the five games and all the practice sessions, Chris did not once show the hesitation in the midst of heated action on the court that might indicate the specter of the tragic accident had returned to haunt him. He was aggressive, almost reckless, in his play.

But that did not mean that the specter ever once left Doug Fulton's mind, even for a second. There were times, both in games and in practice, when he thought for a scary instant that he saw something ominous beginning to develop—a bump, a swinging arm that might connect. But none developed into anything, and Chris seemed never to notice.

Coach Fulton, watching for danger signals through every moment of practice and every moment of every game, finally came to conclude that Chris had shed the burden of his terrible memory. And right behind that, Coach Fulton concluded that nobody ignorant of the true background ever would guess from Chris's play that he had once seriously injured an opponent.

Twice during the two weeks, Doug had visited Brian Patton in his office. He knew that Chris's father appreciated the reports, and Coach Fulton wanted to keep him on his side. He did not need Chris's parents worried any more than necessary about their son playing center for the Panthers.

Both George Holman and Skip Turner had agreed to keep the details of Chris Patton's background in confidence—and they delivered on the promise.

Skip went on the air the morning after Chris's first game with an authoritative recitation of Chris's skills, making it sound as if he was the only person who had noticed the new center and his contributions.

To Skip's credit, he referred to Chris's transfer only once, and then only vaguely, identifying Chris as coming from "an Indiana high school" without specifying the city or the school.

And by the time the next issue of the *Hamilton Weekly Post* came out, Chris's second game with the Panthers was in the record books. George Holman splashed three pictures of Chris in action across the top of the sports page and devoted most of the story to an account of his play in the two games. George, too, identified Chris only as a transfer from "an Indiana high school."

Neither Skip nor George so much as touched the question of why a boy of such obvious skills had not turned out on sign-up day and played for the Panthers from the beginning. Coach Fulton greeted both Skip's broadcast and George Holman's story with sighs of relief.

With the Panthers' steamroller start of the conference schedule, the crowds for both home and away games grew. The Hamilton High gym, frequently a sellout in any season, was packed to standing room only for every game. More and more, Hamilton High fans were making the short road trips to out-of-town games, sometimes outshouting the home team's fans with rhythmic chants of *"Pat-ton"* each time Chris turned and laid the ball in the basket, and *"Al-an"* each time Alan hit the nets with a long shot.

Even Principal Osborne showed up at the games

and a couple of times dropped in on practice, nodding and beaming his approval. Maybe, Coach Fulton figured, the principal was cool toward losers but enjoyed a winner.

As for Doug Fulton, winning felt good, and he decided that waiting three years for his fantasy to come true—a sensational player dropping into his team from out of the blue—was worth the wait.

"Coach, I've got this cousin who lives in Indianapolis. . . ."

Mickey Ward spoke softly, which was out of character, and let the sentence trail off.

Doug and Mickey were alone in the dressing room in the minutes after the last player had departed following the Panthers' decisive victory over the Bunford High Yellowjackets.

Coach Fulton looked at Mickey. The student manager's face wore a troubled expression, as if he was unsure whether to speak. The expression, like the subdued tone of his voice, was unlike the usual confident, upbeat Mickey Ward.

"And . . . ?" Coach Fulton said.

"My cousin goes to Hall High there, and he knows—knew—Chris."

Coach Fulton unconsciously looked around the dressing room to make sure they were alone. Then he said, "Sit down a minute, Mickey."

The boy took a seat on a bench in front of a row of

lockers, and Coach Fulton dropped onto the bench opposite him. The silence in the otherwise empty dressing room was total. Gone were the roaring fans, whose cheers had been heard in the dressing room during halftime. Gone, too, were the celebrating Hamilton High players, who had filled the room with their own cheers only minutes before.

"What about your cousin in Indianapolis, Mickey?" Coach Fulton asked, knowing full well the answer he was going to get.

"We were over in Indianapolis last weekend visiting," the boy said. "My cousin knew that Chris had moved to Hamilton, and he asked about him."

Coach Fulton waited.

Mickey took a deep breath. "He says that Chris played basketball there and—maybe you already know this—that he hit a boy—accidentally, he said—under the basket." Mickey hesitated, watching Coach Fulton. Clearly, the student manager was uncomfortable passing along what might be considered gossip.

"Go on," Coach Fulton said softly.

"And, well, the boy was blind in one eye for a long time. The doctors thought for a while that he was blind for good. You know, permanently. But he got back most of his sight after an operation."

Mickey stopped. Then he asked, "Did you know about that?"

Coach Fulton frowned. "Yes, I know about it," he said, quickly adding, "but I didn't feel at liberty to tell

72

you when we were talking about Chris earlier. I hope you understand."

Mickey nodded. "Sure," he said.

"Have you told anyone about this, Mickey?"

"No. I figured that maybe since nobody had said anything about it, well, maybe Chris didn't want the story getting around."

Yes, Doug thought, Mickey Ward is a very mature young man. To Mickey, he said, "Good. That's right."

"But I thought you ought to know, if you didn't already."

"Yes. Let me explain."

At the finish, Mickey said, "But the accident wasn't Chris's fault. My cousin says everybody knows that. So why doesn't he want it known? There's nothing to be ashamed of."

Coach Fulton shook his head. "I don't know. I agree with you that there's nothing to be ashamed of. All I know is that the accident upset him so much that he was unable to play basketball for almost a year. And he obviously just doesn't want to talk about it. And I—we—should honor his wishes in the matter."

Mickey frowned. "I guess so," he said slowly. He looked up at Coach Fulton. "But if I were Chris, I'd rather have the story of the accident known and be done with it, instead of carrying it around bottled up inside me." He paused. "It's going to get out one of these days, you know. It'd be better for Chris to choose the time and place."

"I think I'd feel the same way, Mickey, but you and I are not Chris Patton."

Mickey said, "Okay," but did not sound as if he was sure of the wisdom of it.

They left the dressing room together and walked down the corridor and out of the building, parting in the darkness as Coach Fulton headed for his car and Mickey turned toward home.

In his car, Doug started the engine, but he sat for a moment before shifting the Volkswagen into first gear. He briefly weighed Mickey's assessment of what Chris should do, then dismissed it. The decision belonged to Chris. Meddling with the boy's decision could only lead to trouble. And he had to admit to himself that he did not want to disturb the carefully balanced circumstances that had allowed Chris to change his mind and play basketball again.

Staring out the windshield at the beams cast by his car's headlights, Coach Fulton pictured Chris going up for a rebound. Chris seemed to have whipped his problem—as long as it remained a secret. Would he be able to control himself if—and when—those around him knew what happened? That question was at the heart of Mickey's idea that Chris should reveal his secret.

As he drove across the parking lot and turned into the street, Coach Fulton counted the number of people around Hamilton who knew—eight, now—and wondered about Chris Patton's reaction when the inevitable leak occurred.

* * *

The next day, Friday, Coach Fulton put the Panthers through a grueling drill to perfect some changes in tactics for the Monday night game at Bakerville. The Spartans, once-beaten and in second place in the Spoon River Conference standings behind Hamilton High, presented the toughest challenge to date for the Panthers, and for Chris Patton at center. The Spartans had their own version of Chris Patton—a tall, strong, very able center. Doug had seen the boy twice last year, when he was a junior, and now he was sure the boy was a little bigger and a little better. Chris was in for a hard battle.

"If you leave their center, Johnson, alone, he'll run wild on you," Coach Fulton had heard on the telephone from a coach whose team had faced the Spartans a few days earlier. "The only way to beat him is to challenge him every time. He tends to foul when pressed—gets frustrated easily and thrashes out. So if you press him hard, maybe he'll foul out."

As a result of that phone call, Doug told Chris: "None of that drifting out around the free throw line. Stay in there under the boards and beat their center. He's big and he's good. But so are you."

He watched Chris as he spoke about a physical battle under the boards: two large and strong players fighting for the ball, time and again. Chris nodded, showing nothing. If the prospect of flying elbows—either giving or receiving blows—bothered him, he gave no indication of it.

To Alan Woodley, Doug said: "You put the ball up there from the outside. They'll have to come out after you, instead of hanging back to help their center with Chris."

And to Bobby Hogan: "Bobby, you take the long shots, too."

With Duddy Ford working against Chris on the boards, the Panthers moved through the plays, over and over again.

And, over and over again, Coach Fulton called out to Chris, "Inside him, get inside him; make him foul you to get to the ball."

Duddy, no match for Chris, did foul repeatedly in his frantic efforts to get around Chris and beat him to a rebound.

Coach Fulton watched and hoped that the Baker-ville center named Johnson would make the same mistake.

Doug Fulton always suffered a mild case of nervousness before an important game. As a player, first in high school and then in college, he never entered a major game without an attack of nerves: a slight shortness of breath, dryness of the mouth, and a feeling akin to being removed from himself, as if he were off to the side, watching. When the action started, the nervousness left—a miraculous cure. The same feelings afflicted him as a coach, and he assumed they always would.

In this case, riding the bus with the players along the darkening highway on the twenty-mile ride to Bakerville, the familiar shortness of breath and dryness of mouth produced a horrible scenario. In Doug Fulton's worst fears, clearly visible in the haze above the road ahead, Alan Woodley missed all—all!—of his outside shots. The Bakerville Spartans, quickly grasping the obvious fact that the little sharp-shooter's aim was off, moved back and ganged up on Chris Patton under the boards. And in the ensuing one-sided battle, it was not the big center named Johnson who fouled out; it was Chris Patton, thrash-ing around, trying to battle the overwhelming odds.

Or worse, Chris, turning furiously, bringing an elbow around . . .

Doug Fulton stopped himself in midthought. But the prospect of Chris accidentally hurting a player in the heat of the action was so terrible that he actually turned around in his seat at the front of the bus, and looked for Chris.

He found him, three rows back on the other side, seated next to Mickey. Chris was smiling and nod-ding at something Mickey was saying, and then they both laughed out loud.

If the Hamilton High Panthers' star center was worried about anything—injuring an opponent, for example, or even the simpler concern about playing the Bakerville Spartans—it wasn't showing.

Coach Fulton glanced at the other faces in the shadows. Each of the players, in his own way, had a method for coping with the nervousness heading into an important game. Bobby Hogan was laughing. Alan Woodley looked as tightly drawn as a violin string. Hubie Willis was listening intently to something Mark Walker was saying, nodding his head solemnly.

As Coach Fulton turned back around to face the windshield again, he reminded himself that the nervousness would vanish when the action began. Well, it always had.

The Bakerville High gymnasium was rapidly filling even as the Hamilton High Panthers trooped down the corridor to their dressing room an hour before game time.

Passing the double doors leading onto the court, Coach Fulton saw a huge red banner with white lettering: Beat Hamilton. He gave a little smile. It was nice to be good enough to be somebody's target and not just another team on the schedule.

In the dressing room, he sat on the training table and watched as Mickey Ward laid things out and the players changed.

There was a quiet about them—even Mickey wasn't saying much—and Coach Fulton wondered if that was good or bad. Good, maybe, if the quiet signified an intensity, a single-minded determination to play the game well. Bad, for sure, if the cause was fear and doubt.

Finally, when the last player was dressed, Coach Fulton came off the training table and stood before them.

"Play your best," he said. "If you play well—every

second of the game—winning will take care of itself. Just play your best."

In the past year, the big center named Johnson had grown a couple more inches and added several pounds of muscle, and he outjumped Chris for the opening tip-off. A square-built little guard grabbed the ball and dribbled in place, giving his teammates a moment to get into position.

Johnson and Chris galloped together toward their positions under the basket.

The Bakerville guard called out something and fired a pass across to the other guard, and the methodical Spartans began weaving their way through an intricate pattern.

Johnson moved with the ball, hands outstretched. Chris stuck with him like a shadow.

The Spartans worked the ball to a forward in the corner and he shot, sending the ball over Marty Townsend's outstretched hands. Johnson and Chris turned with the flight of the ball, poised to leap.

The ball hit the rim and bounced out.

Both Johnson and Chris were in the air. Chris had the better angle. He got a hand on the ball—just his fingertips—and for a long second seemed to be trying to coax it to come his way. Then the ball did. He brought it in with his left hand, clapped his right hand on it, and bent over his prize.

On the bench, Coach Fulton, leaning forward, elbows on his knees, gave a little smile and a short

nod of approval. Chris Patton had won the first skir-
mish in the battle of the boards. The score was Chris
1, Johnson 0.

Coach Fulton's shortness of breath and dryness
of mouth had long since vanished. But he still wanted mightily to see Alan Woodley's first long shot drop
through the net. The horrible scenario in his mind
on the bus ride would linger until Alan hit his first
one. He knew, too, that Alan needed that first basket
to loosen himself up.

On the court, the Spartans were backpedaling
furiously to take up their half-court defense, and
Chris was pivoting with the ball in both hands,
choosing a teammate to receive his pass. He threw
the ball to Bobby Hogan and broke into a run for the
other end of the court.

Bobby dribbled across the center stripe and
flipped the ball across to Alan. Alan dribbled forward
a couple of steps. He looked as if he wanted to shoot
but changed his mind because of two pairs of hands
waggling in front of his face. It was obvious that the
Spartans had received the word on the sophomore
shooter's accuracy from the outside. At least for the
moment, they were double-teaming him when he
had the ball. Alan turned and passed the ball back to
Bobby, breaking toward the basket.

Coach Fulton straightened up, then leaned forward again, elbows back on his knees, hands
clasped. If the Spartans were going to send help
whenever Alan had the ball, somebody was going to

be wide open. In this instance, it was Bobby.

Bobby brought in the pass, dribbled toward the basket, and when Johnson turned to challenge him, palmed a pass to Chris.

Chris was already starting up when he grabbed the ball. Johnson, caught flat-footed, tried to react, but he was too late. Chris was in the air, laying the ball in the basket.

Chris had whipped Johnson again!

Coach Fulton mumbled: "Chris 2, Johnson 0."

Then he mumbled: "But the game is just beginning."

From the opening field goal of the game until halftime, the two teams struggled up and down the court, exchanging the lead eight times, with neither able to stretch a lead to more than three points. The Panthers led, 26–25, when the halftime buzzer sounded.

Coach Fulton got to his feet, glanced at the scoreboard, and turned to walk to the dressing room. As always when walking off the court at halftime, he let the play of the first half pass in review through his mind.

Alan Woodley did get his first long field goal—and his second, third, and fourth. The Panther guard was on the mark, despite the Spartans' tactic of on-again, off-again double-teaming.

Chris was beating Johnson under the boards more often than not. But Johnson was tough, and

Chris was having to call up what was probably his best game ever to stay ahead of the big Bakerville center. Trying to stay inside of him under the basket, Chris had drawn Johnson into committing three fouls in the first half. One more and Johnson would be reduced to caution. Chris himself had two fouls to show for the rough physical battle under the basket, and Coach Fulton made a mental note to remind him of it.

In the dressing room, Coach Fulton took a seat on the training table and gave the players time to towel off and catch their breath.

Chris was dripping wet with sweat, but he had the look of fire in his eyes. He was ready to return to the action. Coach Fulton had seen that look in the eyes of a player before, but only rarely. Chris was one of those players who thrived on competition, who grew stronger in the struggle instead of weary.

Alan and Bobby were seated together, both breathing heavily. Bobby was looking around the room and grinning. Maybe some of the nervousness was still there, and in his case, it was a good thing. Alan was staring blankly at his hands.

Coach Fulton dropped off his perch on the training table and slowly wandered the room, offering encouragement, suggestions, and the occasional criticism to individual players.

Then he walked back to the table, leaned against it, and folded his arms over his chest. "More close games are won in the first few minutes of the second half than at any other time," he said. "The team that comes out of the dressing room and succeeds in putting together a run wins the game. The opening minutes of the second half is the time for us to pull away from them."

The players were watching him—Chris with his head back, stretching his neck muscles, Bobby now with a serious expression, no longer grinning.

"It takes great defense, not just good shooting, to make a run. We've got to score, yes, but then we've got to get the ball back so we can score again. That means creating turnovers—steals, interceptions. Create confusion with tight defense, and they'll throw the ball out of bounds or fumble it away. You've got to force it."

Coach Fulton paused, and the only sound was the low rumble of the crowd from the gymnasium. Then he said, "Okay, let's go."

Coach Fulton got his run.

The second half was barely moments old when Alan hit the net from the edge of the keyhole, then promptly stole the ball from a dribbling Bakerville guard and repeated the feat.

In their next possession, the Spartans got the ball into scoring position only to see a lay-up roll off the edge of the rim and into Chris's hands. Chris sent a pass on a line half the length of the court to Marty Townsend, who beat his pursuers to the goal and laid the ball up for two.

After five minutes, the Hamilton High Panthers had increased their lead to 39–27, and Johnson had drawn his fourth foul. He was sitting on the bench, being saved for the final minutes of the game.

Without Johnson's menacing figure under the boards, Coach Fulton waved Chris out a couple of steps, and Chris promptly delivered a couple of his feather-touch shots from near the free throw line.

When Johnson returned to the court, the Spartans succeeded in putting together a run of their own—eight unanswered points—but it was too little, too late, and Hamilton won, 65–57.

In the noisy dressing room, Coach Fulton took in a deep breath and exhaled, grinned at the players, and told himself: Chris did not foul out; Alan did not miss all his long shots; and Chris did not accidentally injure . . .

He blocked the thought again.

Still grinning, he told himself one more thing: This is going to be a championship team.

If, he added with a slight tilt of the head, nothing goes wrong.

The first snow of the season, a light one, covered the ground the next morning, and Doug Fulton drove slowly over the slippery streets from his apartment to school. The dark skies seemed to warn of more snow before the day was out.

But the gloomy weather and the slosh of the parking lot did nothing to dampen the coach's spirits. He was almost smiling as he pulled into a parking place, got out, and picked his way toward the back door of the school building.

Students with books under their arms were approaching the building from all directions, just ahead of the bell for the opening of the school day.

Coach Fulton saw Mickey Ward a half block away and gave the student manager an exaggerated wave. Mickey returned the greeting.

Inside, Doug walked down the corridor past the gymnasium, turned to his right, unlocked his office door, and stepped in just as the first bell was ringing. That was the warning bell, alerting everyone that five minutes remained before the start of the first class.

He walked around behind his desk, then lifted two sheets of folded paper from the inside pocket of his jacket. Still standing, he unfolded the sheets, laid them flat on the desk, and stared at them. He was still looking at the pages, bending over to make an occasional notation in pencil, when the bell rang for the first class.

No matter how good the game, no matter how well the team had played, there was always room for improvement, there were always mistakes to be corrected. And these notes jotted in his apartment before going to bed the night before told the flip-side story of the Hamilton Panthers' victory over the Bakerville Spartans.

Doug had not mentioned shortcomings and errors in the dressing room. That was the time for enjoying the wonderful figures on the scoreboard at the finish of the game. Nor had he offered any suggestions or criticisms to any player on the bus ride back home. That, too, was a time for savoring victory. So was the rest of the evening in the home of each player.

But now it was Tuesday, the day after the game, and a practice session was coming up in the afternoon. These notes on the miscues and might-havebeens of the Bakerville game were going to be the points of emphasis on the practice court.

While the players were going to their classes, still smiling in the wonderful glow of the victory, enjoying the calls of congratulations, Coach Fulton was working on a way to make them even better.

He changed quickly into his gym shoes and walked out to greet the boys in his first-period gym class. The notes would have to wait until his open period.

"Coach?"

Coach Fulton looked up from his desk. In his concentration, he had not been aware of the student stepping through his door and now standing in front of his desk. He recognized the boy's face but could not recall his name.

"Yes," he said.

"This is from Mr. Osborne," the boy said, placing an envelope on the desk.

The boy was one of the students who worked in Hamilton High's administrative office during one classroom period each day, collecting attendance records and running errands. The selection of students for the assignments was based on grades because the student worker had to sacrifice a study hall. It was something of an honor to be chosen.

Suddenly the boy's name came into Coach Fulton's mind, and he said, "Thanks, Ned."

The student left, and Doug opened the envelope and withdrew a handwritten note: *Please come to my office during your open period.* It was signed with Principal Osborne's initials: J.O.

Well, this was the open period, so Coach Fulton got up and walked out of his office.

"Why didn't you tell me about Chris Patton's past problems?"

Principal Osborne was seated behind the desk in his office.

Coach Fulton was in the stuffed chair in front of the desk. He glanced through the open door of the office. A girl at the telephone switchboard was the only person visible. Doug looked back at Principal Osborne and, nodding his head toward the door, said, "May I?"

"All right."

Coach Fulton got up and walked to the door. He saw Mary at her desk, her back to him, and the other office workers. He closed the door and returned to the chair. He did not speak for a moment. The principal's tone, as well as the term "Chris Patton's past problems," troubled him.

He chose his words carefully. "Are you referring to the accident he was involved in?"

"A rather serious accident, I think you'll agree."

"Yes, the boy was blinded in one eye for a time, until he had surgery."

There was a moment of silence, and Coach

Fulton knew that Principal Osborne was waiting for an answer to his opening question. The coach wanted to say, "Principal Osborne, until our recent wins, you've never shown much interest in athletics in general and in basketball in particular. So you and I seldom have reason to converse. That is why I never mentioned Chris Patton's background in casual conversation. As for making a point of informing you, I did not think that was necessary, and I had no reason to believe you would be interested."

But instead, all that Doug Fulton said was, "I did not think it necessary."

"Didn't you think I would be interested in the fact that a boy who blinded an opposing player last year was now playing for Hamilton High?"

Doug Fulton felt a rising wave of anger—an unusual emotion for him—and he took a couple of breaths before replying. "It's not as if he committed a crime. It was an accident—tragic, but still an accident."

"These things can be very dangerous for a school, you know."

Yes, Doug Fulton knew. Somebody might sue somebody. It was always happening, it seemed. It was why Hamilton High, like other schools, required a waiver signed by a parent for every boy or girl on any athletic team. He said, "Chris Patton represents no more danger to Hamilton High than any other student."

The principal leaned back in his chair, watching

Coach Fulton. Then he said, "I understand he did not come out for the team until after the season had started."

"That's correct."

"Why was that?"

"He was terribly torn up by the accident, as you can understand. He quit his team in Indianapolis after it happened. He thought he was through with basketball forever. Then he changed his mind."

"Did you talk him into coming out for the team?"

"No."

Principal Osborne waited a moment, seemingly expecting Coach Fulton to amend his flat statement.

Doug felt the anger rising again. Principal Osborne seemed to be coming close to accusing him of actively recruiting a monster who would injure opposing players on the basketball court. But he said nothing. The no was true, and he let it stand.

"Did you know about this incident when he decided to come out for the team?"

"Yes," Doug said, and explained his telephone call to Coach Barnes at Hall High in Indianapolis.

"And you accepted him without question, even though you knew of this serious problem in his background?"

The anger broke through this time, and Coach Fulton did not try to stop it. "Are you leading up to saying that I should expel Chris Patton from the team because of an accident that occurred last year?"

Principal Osborne glared at him a moment.

That's exactly what he wants to say, Coach Fulton thought, because he thinks there is a chance that Chris Patton really is dangerous on the basketball court. But maybe—probably—he won't say it.

After another moment, Principal Osborne said, "Are you absolutely certain in your own mind that the incident was wholly accidental?"

Coach Fulton almost sighed audibly with relief. "After speaking with Coach Barnes in Indianapolis, yes, I am certain." He paused. "And furthermore, Chris's father, Brian Patton, told me that the boy who was injured—the boy and his parents—accepted that it was a tragic accident and nothing more."

Principal Osborne nodded his head slowly, keeping his eyes on Coach Fulton, and said, "All right. If you're certain."

"I'm certain," Coach Fulton said.

The principal made a move to get to his feet, signaling that the interview was at an end.

"Just a moment, please," Coach Fulton said.

Principal Osborne settled back. "What?"

"None of the players know about Chris's accident. It seems he prefers it that way, for his own reasons. He's never mentioned it, even to me, and I've of course never mentioned it to him. I've spoken with his father about it—at his father's invitation—but that's about all." Doug hesitated, knowing he was leaving out more than a couple of people. But the

92

point was that he did not want the subject to become corridor chatter. "I hope that you will not need to mention the accident to anyone, at least as long as Chris wants it kept quiet."

"All right." Principal Osborne made a move toward getting up again.

"One other thing, if I may."

"Yes."

"With Chris's history of the accident being more or less a secret—where did you hear about it?"

Principal Osborne eyed Coach Fulton for a moment before he replied. Then he said, "At the game last night in Bakerville. I happened to wind up seated next to Chris's parents." He paused briefly and added, "The Pattons seemed to assume that I would have known about Chris from you."

Coach Fulton nodded, understanding that he had left the principal wide open for what could have been an embarrassing moment. "I'm sorry," he said. "I'll keep you advised."

"Thank you."

At the start of practice, the players were still riding high with the memory of their important triumph over the Bakerville Spartans. All the signs were there during the warm-up shots. Bobby Hogan joked with a crazy-legged dribble before shooting, and everyone hooted. Even Chris, normally serious in practice, toyed with Alan Woodley, holding the ball high above the sharpshooter's outstretched hands instead of letting it drop.

Then Coach Fulton called the players around him.

"Folks," he said with a smile, "we're going to talk about mistakes."

It wasn't the first time that Coach Fulton had opened the structured portion of practice with that kind of statement. But it might well have been. The players responded with questioning looks.

"And we'll begin with you, Chris," he said.

The Panthers marched not only unbeaten but almost unthreatened past their next three opponents. They whipped Chandler High, 65–53, then crushed Haney High, 66–47, and trampled Danielville High, 59–46.

In that period, the Bakerville Spartans suffered a second loss in the Spoon River Conference. Although they still clung to second place in the standings, the Spartans no longer were breathing down the Panthers' necks. Hamilton High was not only in first place, but firmly so.

Alan Woodley's deadly outside shooting led the scoring, but it was Chris Patton at center who really made the difference. On the rare occasions when Alan missed, he frequently got a second chance right away because Chris grabbed the rebound and shot a pass back to him. Alan owed not a few of his points to the second chances provided by Chris. It became a running joke with Chris. The boy, so confident of his own ability and also of Alan's, frequently fired off the pass to Alan with a grinning call, "Here, try it again." Then, when Alan scored on the second shot, Chris called out, "That's better."

Chris did not always bring down a rebound and pass it off to Alan. A lot of his rebounds ended with the ball dropping through the net, deftly tipped by the leaping Chris. Unlike the popular scenes of professional basketball players slamming the ball through the net, Chris dealt lightly, almost delicately, with the ball. So much so, in fact, that sometimes Coach Fulton could not discern that Chris had even touched the ball. It seemed almost as if the boy had willed the ball into the basket. But, of course, Chris had touched the ball. Coach Fulton knew that a basketball did not reverse direction in midair without somebody doing something.

Along the way, Coach Fulton gradually changed the style of the Panthers' play to take fuller advantage of Chris's abilities. Chris was quicker in moving down the length of the court than Duddy Ford. And he tried harder. So with Chris's abilities to build on, Coach Fulton speeded up the tempo of the Panthers' game.

Chris's ability to rifle a one-handed pass three-quarters the length of the court, much like a shortstop throwing a baseball to first base, gave the

Panthers an unexpected weapon in their arsenal. Neither Duddy nor most other high school players could do it. The first time Coach Fulton had seen Chris palm the ball, cock his arm, and send a pass on a line down the court, he stopped the practice and said, "Chris, do that again." Chris grinned and did it again. The pass became the heart of a new play that, again, speeded up the tempo of the Panthers' attack. When Chris came down with a rebound in his hands, Hubie Willis, Mark Walker, or Marty Townsend would break into a dead run for the basket, bring in Chris's rocketlike pass, dribble once, and lay the ball up.

The changing style of the Panthers' offense left Duddy Ford spending more and more time on the bench. The team's attack now relied so heavily on Chris's skills that their entire style of play changed when Chris was not in the game. Coach Fulton knew that Duddy was disgruntled—and, yes, even embarrassed—by his rare appearances on the court, usually at the end of a game already won. But Duddy said nothing, and neither did Coach Fulton. Presumably, Duddy knew that Chris was the better player. Duddy's role was to wait in case he was needed. To wait, to be ready, in the event that Chris got in foul trouble, or Chris got hurt, or . . .

Coach Fulton always stopped himself from finishing that thought, but the fact remained that Chris's problem—Chris's secret—was never long out of his mind.

Through all of the picture-perfect practice sessions and all of the overwhelming victories, Coach Fulton constantly felt a gnawing dread of the moment when something might come leaping out of Chris's past to make everything go wrong.

Mickey's point—that Chris should choose a time and place and let the secret be known—kept coming back into Coach Fulton's mind.

It was a Friday.

Coach Fulton ran the Panthers through less than an hour of an easy practice and sent them to the showers.

"Enjoy the weekend," he told them.

The players had worked hard these first weeks of the season. First, they struggled with Duddy Ford's shortcomings at center. Then, they adjusted to a new center in the person of Chris Patton. And, finally, they had succeeded in mastering changes in their style of play. A day off from the strain of a long full-speed practice session would do them good.

In addition, their opponents on Monday night were to be the hapless Barrington Bulldogs, who were winners of only one game so far in the season. Coach Fulton allowed himself the rare luxury of absolute confidence. His front-running Panthers were going to have no trouble with the almost winless Bulldogs.

He saw the last of the players out of the dressing room, watched a minute as Mickey made a final sweep gathering up towels going to the laundry, and said, "I've got an appointment downtown." Then he left, reminding Mickey to lock up.

At the back door, he peered out at the weather. A heavy rain was falling from a dark gray sky. He buttoned up his topcoat, reminded himself again that he needed to keep an umbrella in his office, and plunged out.

Fifteen minutes later the secretary was ushering him through the outer office into Brian Patton's office.

"Hey, coach," Brian Patton said, getting to his feet.

"It's been a while," Coach Fulton said, extending his right hand across the desk and grasping Mr. Patton's hand.

They sat down.

"I see you twice a week—at every game," Mr. Patton said. "But you don't see me. It always seems you're sort of busy."

Coach Fulton smiled. "I know you would call me if there were any signs of a problem. . . ." He let the sentence trail off.

"Yes, of course. Everything looks fine on the home front." Then Chris's father frowned and asked, "Is there something wrong?"

"Not exactly wrong, no. But, you know, Chris hasn't told anyone about the accident. Or, at least, anyone that I know of. He's never mentioned it to me."

"That bothers you?"

"Only to the extent that we can be sure that somebody someday is going to blow the secret wide open. And it bothers me that it might be the wrong person, and that it might have a devastating effect on Chris. The word is sure to get around. Our student manager, Mickey Ward, for example, learned about it from a cousin who lives in Indianapolis. We can trust Mickey. But who knows about someone else?"

"Mickey Ward? I know him. He's been at our house. Chris spends a lot of time at his house. Mickey's a close friend, probably Chris's closest friend."

"Oh?" Coach Fulton was surprised. He remembered Mickey saying that he had a couple of classes with Chris and that Chris was friendly. He recalled Chris and Mickey sitting together on the team bus; a couple of times, he had seen them eating lunch together in the cafeteria. But he had thought little of these scenes and wasn't aware a close friendship had developed. Maybe, he thought, the coach of the Panthers spent too much of his concentration on dribbling, shooting, and rebounding. Maybe the coach should notice more of the things happening off the court.

"Go on," Mr. Patton said, frowning. "You were concerned that somebody might say something. Like who? And what?"

"Maybe I'm seeing ghosts, worrying about something that's not worth worrying about. But, for example, there might be somebody in the bleachers at a road game—somebody who, perhaps like Mickey, has a cousin in Indianapolis, and has heard the story—and the person shouts something at Chris on the court."

Mr. Patton nodded. "I see."

"People can be cruel sometimes—more cruel than they realize, and . . ."

"Yes." Brian Patton paused. "But isn't that an argument for Chris keeping the secret, rather than letting everyone know?"

"Perhaps. But I'm concerned about Chris being shocked and confused if anything like this happened. His teammates wouldn't have any idea what had happened, and they wouldn't be in any position to support him. Chris wouldn't even know that I know."

"Do you want me to talk to him?"

Coach Fulton waited a moment before replying: Then he said, "I came here this afternoon planning to suggest that I talk to Chris, explain that I know about the accident, and urge him to at least tell his teammates—or, if you felt strongly about it, that you do the talking." He paused. "But now I've got another idea."

"Yes?"

"Mickey Ward."

Mr. Patton frowned. Then he said, "Chris may have told Mickey."

"I don't think so. Mickey came to me right away with the story he heard in Indianapolis. I told him to keep it to himself, and he has. If Chris had told him about the accident, I think Mickey would have let me know." He gave a little smile. "No," he added, "I think those two boys are walking around keeping the same secret from each other—Chris because he finds it painful to face up to the story, and Mickey because he figures this is the way his friend wants it."

"Maybe."

"Either way, Mickey can talk with Chris as a friend—one boy to another—more effectively than an adult can, even if that adult is the father or the coach."

"You put a lot of stock in Mickey Ward."

"Mickey is very special, as Chris probably recognizes."

"Will Mickey want to do this?"

Coach Fulton smiled. "Actually, it was Mickey's idea that Chris ought to tell his secret and sort of get the monkey off his back. I just didn't recognize it as a good idea when Mickey first mentioned it."

Downstairs in the building lobby, Doug stepped into a telephone booth and thumbed through a pocket notebook until he found Mickey Ward's home phone number. He could catch him now, maybe, before Mickey went out for the Friday evening. Then Mickey could talk to Chris, tonight or over the weekend. He dialed the number.

Mickey's mother answered the telephone. No, Mrs. Ward said, Mickey was not there. He and his father had left as soon as Mickey got home from school. They were spending the weekend at the Wards' cabin near Lake Shelbyville. It was their last chance for a fishing trip before winter set in. She could reach him by calling a gasoline station a half mile from the cabin, if this was an emergency.

"No, no," Coach Fulton said. "Nothing urgent at all. It will wait until next week."

The Panthers raced to a 10–2 lead in the opening minutes against the Barrington Bulldogs, and already Coach Fulton was thinking of starting the process of pulling out the starters and sending substitutes onto the court.

The pitiful Bulldogs lacked everything: skill, height, strength. They were poor shooters, inept dribblers, ineffective rebounders. Coach Fulton knew that it could happen to any high school. This simply was not a year when the student body of Barrington High included five—or even one or two—good basketball players. He sympathized with Coach Borden Dailey. He was a good coach, sitting morosely on the Barrington High bench, suffering his way through another terrible game in a miserable season.

Only a smattering of fans had turned out on this wintry Monday night in Barrington. They were parents and close friends, undoubtedly. Nobody else wanted to watch the Bulldogs take another hammering.

In glancing over the bleachers during the pre-game warm-up, Coach Fulton had not seen a single familiar face from Hamilton. The Panthers' fans, while excited about their team's winning ways, had decided to skip the drive to Barrington in bad weather for a certain runaway game played out by substitutes.

At the scorer's table, Skip Turner sat, leaning forward, chattering into his microphone. The smaller the turnout of fans at the game, the larger his radio audience—if he could contrive a way to make a rout of the Barrington Bulldogs interesting enough to hold his listeners.

Coach Fulton got to his feet at the sideline and prepared to send Duddy in for Chris, Mark Walker in for Marty Townsend, and maybe one other second-stringer.

On the court, a Barrington player was struggling to break free of Bobby Hogan and put the ball up. Finally, he got the shot away. It was off the mark to the left and hit the rim and then the backboard and went up.

Under the basket, Chris had his face turned to the ceiling. He was watching the ball and positioning himself to leap at the proper instant. The ball was coming down now, and Chris sprung into the air.

A Barrington player made a frantic leap in front of him.

Chris, his eyes on the ball above, his hands reaching high, never saw the Barrington player until they collided.

The thinner Barrington player bounced off Chris's sturdy frame like a tennis ball off a brick wall; he flew backward toward the floor. He landed on his back with a thump and his head hit the court with a cracking sound.

Coach Fulton turned from the players on the bench with the collision and saw it all.

The Barrington player did not move.

Chris, the ball held in two hands, stood motionless, staring at the form sprawled on the court. Then he turned a face with an expression of horror toward the Hamilton High bench.

For an instant, nobody on the court moved; all were frozen.

Then it seemed everybody was moving—everybody except the boy sprawled on the court under the basket.

Coach Dailey leaped off the Barrington High bench and rushed to the fallen player.

Mickey Ward was first off the Hamilton High bench, and he reached the stunned Chris a moment before Coach Fulton.

One of the officials tried to step in front of Doug. "Stay off the court, coach," he said.

"Shut up," Coach Fulton said, and pushed his way past.

When he reached Chris, Mickey already had an

arm around his waist and was saying, "C'mon, Chris, let's go to the bench for a minute."

Coach Dailey was bending over the inert player. A man in a suit, possibly a doctor, came down out of the bleachers and ran onto the court and joined Coach Dailey.

Chris said loudly, "No." It was almost a scream. He dropped the ball and clenched his fists in front of him.

Coach Fulton thought at first that Chris was going to take a swing at Mickey, who, his arm still around Chris's waist, was trying to propel him toward the bench.

Chris shouted again, "No!"

Coach Fulton didn't know whether Chris meant, "No, I'm not going to the bench," or "No, this can't possibly have happened."

He moved around in front of the boy. "Chris," he said softly, "I know all about it."

"You—what?"

Coach Fulton did not answer. He knew that Chris was fully aware of what he had said, and what the words meant. The awareness was written on Chris's face, along with surprise.

"We've got to all"—the coach emphasized the word *all*—"go to the bench now, and wait and see what the situation is." He took Chris's arm in his right hand and, without making any move to push or pull him, turned to Mickey. Speaking loudly enough to be sure that Chris heard him, he said, "Round up all our players and get them to the bench."

Beyond Mickey, Coach Fulton saw the boy on the floor moving his hands and legs. He seemed to be trying to sit up. He let out a low groan.

Coach Fulton tightened his grip on Chris's arm and led him to the bench. Mickey and the other players followed.

By the time they reached the bench, the Barrington player was struggling to his feet and rubbing the back of his head. He even had a little grin on his face, as if asking, "What happened?"

"He's okay, I think," Coach Fulton said.

Chris turned and looked. The Barrington player was making his way shakily to the bench with the help of Coach Dailey and the man from the bleachers.

The referee was trying to get the action going again.

"Give it a minute, will you?" Coach Fulton snapped at the official. Then he turned to Chris. "C'mon, let's go see how the boy is."

Chris nodded and followed Coach Fulton down the sideline, past the scorer's table, toward the Barrington High bench.

"I'm calling a technical on you, coach," the official called out to Doug Fulton's back.

"Call all the technicals you like," the coach replied.

When Doug and Chris reached the Barrington High bench, the player was saying, "I'm all right, I'm all right." The man in the suit was bent over in front of him, staring intently at the boy's eyes and doing something that seemed like testing his focus.

Coach Fulton and Chris stood and watched for a moment, saying nothing.

Then the man straightened up and said, "Mainly, he had the breath knocked out of him. He bumped his head, but I don't see any signs of concussion."

Chris said, "I'm sorry. I didn't mean . . ."

The boy grinned at Chris. "No problem. I'm okay now."

As Doug and Chris walked back to the Hamilton High bench, Chris said, "I don't want to play anymore."

Coach Fulton looked at him. Did Chris mean he did not want to play anymore tonight? Or ever? Finally the coach said, "No, all of the starters are coming to the bench."

When play resumed, Coach Fulton sat on the bench next to Chris, with the other starters—Bobby, Alan, all of them—strung out along the bench to their right. Duddy Ford and the other second-stringers were on the court facing the Barrington High Bulldogs.

"Are your parents here tonight?" Coach Fulton asked. "I haven't seen them."

"No." Chris kept his eyes on the action on the

court. "My father had a late meeting, and with the lousy weather and all, well, I told them that Duddy was probably going to play most of the game, anyway."

"Uh-huh."

They watched as a Barrington High player fumbled a pass and let it bounce out of bounds.

"There's the boy going back in the game," Coach Fulton said. "He's all right."

Chris leaned forward and looked down the sideline, watching the boy check in at the scorer's table and then walk onto the court. He said, "Yeah," and the word sounded flat. The small crowd gave the boy a smattering of applause.

They watched in silence for a few minutes, and the Panthers ran their lead to 18–6. Then Chris turned to Coach Fulton. "What did you mean when you said that you knew all about it?"

Coach Fulton kept his eyes straight ahead, concentrating on Duddy Ford's try and miss on a hook shot. He had known that Chris was going to ask the question. Either here on the bench, in the dressing room at halftime, after the game, on the bus riding back to Hamilton, or tomorrow in practice. Chris had understood Coach Fulton's statement, even in the intense emotion of the moment. He was bound to ask.

"I know about your accident at Hall High," Doug said, keeping his gaze on the players on the court. "I've known from the beginning."

Chris frowned. "How?"

"Coach Barnes. I called him about you, after you told me that you weren't a basketball player. I was sure you were."

"You never said anything about it."

Coach Fulton turned to Chris, smiled, and said, "Neither did you."

When their eyes met, Doug wanted to ask, "What did you mean when you said you didn't want to play anymore?" But he didn't ask. He didn't want to press for an answer right now, barely minutes after the emotional shock of seeing the unmoving player lying on his back on the floor. No, better to wait. There would be a better chance of getting the right answer later.

The first half ended with the Panthers leading 36–17, and the players trooped to the dressing room.

Coach Fulton's suggestions and criticisms left no doubt that the second-stringers were going to start the second half and probably play through to the finish. He critiqued Duddy's play, lacing his remarks heavily with encouraging praise for his hard work. Next Mark's, and then the others', virtually ignoring Chris and Bobby and the other starters.

They were ready to return to the court when Chris asked, "Okay if I dress now?"

Coach Fulton stared hard at the boy. Thoughts raced crazily through his mind. Was this a result of Chris not wanting to play again? Tonight? Or forever?

Doug let the silence hang between them for only a moment. "No," he said. "It would be the height of insult to have any of our starters not even dress for the second half. We're not going to do that."

As they walked back to the court and the almost-empty bleachers, Coach Fulton toyed with the idea of abruptly turning to Chris at some point in the second half and ordering him into the game.

But even before he reached the bench and took his seat to watch the warm-up shots, he decided not to. It was too chancy.

The end of the game finally came. The Panthers won by a score of 59–41.

The bus was pulling into the Hamilton High parking lot. Its headlights were shining on the back of the school building. The rain, which had stopped when the team emerged from the Barrington High gym to board the bus, began falling again halfway home and now was a light drizzle.

Several cars were parked in the lot—friends and family, there to pick up the returning players. Other cars followed the bus onto the lot, driven by the few fans who had made the trip to Barrington for the game. They, too, would be picking up players to go home. Coach Fulton required the players to ride the bus back to the school from road games, even if they had family or friends with a car offering a ride. He did not relish the idea of receiving a midnight telephone call from parents wondering why their son was not home.

When the bus came to a halt, Coach Fulton stood up from his seat in the front, turned, and gazed the length of the bus as the interior lights went on. He spotted Chris, seated again with Mickey, near the back. There was no laughter and joking this time. Both were staring somberly ahead. Then they began getting to their feet and sliding out of their seats into the aisle.

Coach Fulton turned and stepped down from the bus, taking a position by the door in the light drizzling rain.

As the players filed out and walked past him, he watched them head for their car rides home. He had, on occasion, had to take home a player whose ride, for whatever reason, failed to show up.

When Mickey stepped down, Coach Fulton said only, "Good night, Mickey," and sent him on his way.

Behind Mickey, Chris stepped down. Doug tapped him on the arm and said, "A minute, Chris. Wait." Chris stopped and stood next to Coach Fulton while the few remaining players debarked.

"Who's picking you up? Your parents?"

"Yes."

"Do you see their car?"

"There." He gestured in the direction of a car with its headlights on.

"Let's go."

"What? You don't need to . . ."

But Coach Fulton was already leading the way. He hoped he would not find Chris's mother alone in the car. He wanted a brief word with Chris's father.

He saw through the windshield that both parents were in the car, with Brian Patton at the wheel.

While Chris went to the passenger side and got into the backseat, Coach Fulton went around to the driver's side. Mr. Patton rolled down the window. His expression left no doubt that he feared the worst.

"It's okay," Coach Fulton said almost instinctively. "But we had a real scare with a collision under the boards. Chris can tell you about it, and we can talk later."

Chris's father nodded, and Coach Fulton turned and jogged through the drizzling rain to his car.

Doug peeled off his damp clothes and pulled on a robe. Then he went into the kitchenette and put on the teakettle. On a cold and rainy night, a cup of hot tea seemed like a good idea. He stood in front of the stove while the water heated, his mind rerunning Chris's collision with the Barrington player. Doug, on the bench, had felt his heart skip a beat and then sink. He could imagine Chris's immediate reaction. The boy had not leaped to the aid of the fallen player as some players might have done. Instead, he had turned away, as if he could not stand the prospect of looking at the boy. That was a bad sign. Chris had cried out, not for the hurt player, but for himself—

his own agony. That was a bad sign, too.

How can you win the game by eighteen points and then see nothing but bad signs?

The kettle began to whistle, and he poured boiling water over a tea bag in a mug, then carried the mug across his living room to his desk and put it down. He sat at the desk, looking at the phone a moment, then flicked his notebook open to the page he needed, and dialed.

Mickey Ward answered. "I thought it might be you," he said. Then he added, "This looks bad."

"What did Chris say?"

"Just that he's quitting. And that he never should have come back to basketball in the first place."

Coach Fulton nodded silently to himself. "Anything else?"

Mickey did not speak for a moment. "I told him that I knew about the accident in Indianapolis," he said finally. Then he added quickly, "I know I promised, but, well, it seemed to me that the situation had changed, and—"

"You did the right thing. You were right to tell him. What did he say?"

"He seemed kind of relieved that I knew, and he told me all about it. Nothing I didn't already know, really, except . . ."

"Except what?"

"Well, he was sort of doubly torn up by the whole thing."

"What do you mean?"

"Well, the accident was bad, really bad. Everyone thought the boy was permanently blind in one eye. All that Chris could think about was that he was the one who had done it. Then the boy missed a whole semester of school when they operated on him. It was a bad scene. For Chris, too, I mean."

"Yes, I know. And he relived it all in a horrible moment tonight. But what do you mean by 'doubly torn up'?"

"Basketball was his whole life, and when he decided to quit then, that was the end of it. He had all sorts of plans—dreams, you know—maybe winning the state championship, making the all-state team, going on to play in college. And it all came tumbling down." Mickey paused. "I guess that's why he decided to give it another try this year."

"Yes, I can understand. Let me know if you talk to him again. I'm interested."

"What are you going to do?"

"Right now, I'm just going to wait. Wait and see what he wants to do. And then go along with his decision."

"He ought to play, to beat this thing."

"We'll see, Mickey."

"And I told him so."

"We'll have to wait and see."

Coach Fulton hung up the telephone and sat, his hand still on the receiver. Sure, Chris ought to play—and beat this thing, as Mickey said. Surely Chris felt the same way, or he never would have come out for the Hamilton High team. But the horrible memory was still there, brought to the surface by a collision tonight.

Then the telephone rang under Coach Fulton's hand.

"Doug?"

"Yes." He knew who it was.

"Brian here."

"Yes." Despite his hopes, he felt a sense of resignation more than anything else.

"Chris is determined to quit. He's quite adamant. I'll have to go along with him, of course."

"Of course. So will I. I'm sorry, but it is his decision."

Coach Fulton did not go to his office when he arrived at Hamilton High the next morning. Instead, still wearing his raincoat, he went straight to the administrative office. The warning bell was only a couple of minutes from ringing, which meant the first class was six or seven minutes away.

Mary was not at her desk, nor anywhere in the office.

Coach Fulton was looking around for someone else to help him when she walked in, closing her umbrella.

"Take off your coat and stay a while," she said with a smile. Then she added, "Uh-oh, your face looks bleaker than the weather."

"Chris had an accident in the game at Barrington

last night. Nothing serious, but it hit him hard, and he's quitting the team."

"Oh, no. Was somebody hurt?"

"Not badly, no." He explained briefly what had happened.

Mary frowned. "I'm sorry."

"Yeah. I want to see him before his first class. Can you look up his schedule for me?"

"Sure." She walked to a file cabinet and pulled open a drawer. Thumbing through folders, she extracted one, glanced inside, and said, "Mr. Emerson's English composition. Do you know where Mr. Emerson's classroom is?"

"Sure. Thanks." He turned to go, then turned back. With a nod toward the closed door to Mr. Osborne's office, he said, "I want to see him during the second period. It's my open period. Give me a call when he can see me, will you?"

Mary nodded. "Sure."

Coach Fulton walked out of the office and through the lobby into a stairwell. Going up the stairs, he slipped off his raincoat and carried it over his arm. He hurried through the crowd of students in the corridor, heading toward the classroom at the far end. When he arrived, he looked in. No Chris Patton. He stepped back into the corridor.

Chris, approaching, spotted Coach Fulton waiting outside Mr. Emerson's classroom and looked for all the world as if he wanted to turn and run.

Coach Fulton smiled at Chris and walked toward him. The boy stopped and waited for him, his mouth a thin line, his jaw clenched, appearing to brace himself for the inevitable. His expression seemed to say, "Well, I might as well get this over with now."

"Your father called me last night," Coach Fulton said.

"I know."

"I just wanted to tell you that I understand."

The hard look on Chris's face softened. Doug realized, with something of a jolt, that Chris probably was expecting him to try to talk him out of his decision.

"Thanks," Chris said finally. "I hope that the others . . ."

"They'll understand, too. I'll tell them the whole story at practice this afternoon. They'll understand."

The bell rang for the first class, but Chris just stood there, making no move to enter the classroom.

Coach Fulton feared for a moment that he was going to see tears well up in Chris's eyes. Maybe accosting him in the corridor before class had been a bad idea. But Doug wanted to have his words of understanding spoken before he encountered Chris in another, even less appropriate, setting.

"I'm sorry," Chris said.

Coach Fulton mustered a smile. "I'm sorry, too." Then, without thinking, he added, "If you change your mind, your spot will be open."

Chris nodded without speaking and walked into the classroom.

Coach Fulton, ignoring the puzzled stares of students in the corridor, turned and hurried downstairs to greet his first-period gym class.

Mickey Ward was waiting in the corridor when Coach Fulton reached his office after class. "He's quitting, isn't he?"

Coach Fulton got his key out of his pocket and opened the door. "Yes," he said. He walked in and Mickey followed. "Aren't you supposed to be in class?"

"It's study hall, and you can give me a note. Chris shouldn't quit."

Coach Fulton blinked at Mickey's blithe explanation of how to cut a class, followed by his quick return to the subject of the visit. As Doug walked around his desk and sat down, Mickey dropped into the chair at the side of the desk, uninvited. The student manager was going to grow up to be a lawyer, maybe governor of the state, Coach Fulton guessed with a small grin.

"I don't think he should quit," Coach Fulton said, "and you don't think he should quit. Even his father would prefer that he not quit. But Chris thinks he should, and it's his decision."

Mickey weighed Coach Fulton's words for a moment and then said, "We can't just let him quit."

Doug said, "Mickey, there's a lot more involved

121

than winning the championship. Sometimes things are—"

"That's what I'm talking about. Not the championship, but Chris being a quitter, going through the rest of his life wondering if he could have whipped this thing, if only his last chance wasn't gone." Mickey looked at Coach Patton. "This is Chris's last chance."

Coach Fulton took a deep breath. He waited a moment, marveling once again at the maturity of his student manager. Then he said, "Chris's father is going along with Chris's decision. I have no choice but to do the same." He paused and then added, "And neither do you."

Mickey frowned and finally said, "I'll give this some thought."

Coach Fulton grinned at Mickey's determined expression and said, "Well, do it quietly, please, until I've had a chance to tell the players at practice. And do it in your study hall, where you ought to be right now. I'll write you a tardiness excuse—this time."

Coach Fulton closed the door behind Mickey and returned to his chair. He pulled it back, sat down, and lifted his feet onto the desk. Clasping his hands behind his head, he stared at the opposite wall.

Mickey was right, of course. But equally right was that the decision was Chris's to make.

Doug had not talked Chris into coming out for the team in the first place, and he was glad of it. It had been Chris's decision, arrived at without any shoving from a coach who could be accused of wanting to win a championship no matter the cost. No, Doug was sure he had done the right thing then, and he was determined to do the right thing now.

He frowned as his mind went back to his remark to Chris—"If you change your mind"—and wondered if the boy might construe it as pressure. No, surely not. It was an invitation and would be interpreted as such. He did not intend to pressure, and he would not apply pressure. It was Chris's decision.

But Chris was turning his back on a great senior season at Hamilton High, as well as an excellent prospect of a brilliant college career. He was a cinch to be named to the all-conference team. He might even be named to the all-state team. With his ability and size, major colleges all over the country would be interested in Chris Patton. He would have his pick of the schools. But instead, because of the memory of a dreadful accident, there were not going to be any all-conference or maybe even all-state honors for Chris Patton. And there was going to be no major college basketball career, nor a victory or two in the NCAA tournament.

Coach Fulton remembered when his college team twice won the right to play in the NCAA tournament, going to the final sixteen before losing in his senior season. It was the thrill of a lifetime, a thrill that Chris Patton could know but never would.

For sure, Chris understood the thrill that goes

with being a good basketball player on a good team. The understanding was written all over his face during every practice and every game—every tip-in, every rebound, every shot from fifteen feet out, every steal. The thrill of the game had been written on his face, until that Barrington High player foolishly leaped into him going up for the ball. Then there had been no thrilled look on Chris Patton's face. Coach Fulton remembered the look. It had been one of horror.

The telephone on his desk rang. He brought down his feet and answered it. Mary Corliss told him that Principal Osborne was in his office and available.

"We're lucky, I guess, that it wasn't worse," Principal Osborne said. He was seated at his desk.

Coach Fulton was in the stuffed chair. "Yes, of course," he said.

The principal made a pyramid of his fingers in front of his chin. "Unfortunate," he said, as if speaking to himself. Then he looked at Coach Fulton. "The boy really is a superior player, isn't he?"

"Yes, I think he's one of the best I've ever seen at the high school level."

"I checked his grades. They're good."

"I'm not surprised. He's a fine young man."

"Well, yes. Well, thank you for filling me in."

Doug got to his feet. "Of course."

* * *

The coach sat on the training table and watched the players arrive for practice. He wondered if any of them knew of Chris's decision. Probably not. He couldn't imagine Chris telling anyone, because that would lead to questions—and the need for an explanation of his painful background. Chris would leave that up to the coach.

When the last player—save for Chris Patton—was in the dressing room, Coach Fulton slid off the training table and stood at the side of the dressing room. He wanted to be able to see all the players as he spoke.

In front of him, the first arrivals were almost dressed in their practice uniforms and the later arrivals were still in their street clothes.

By now some of them had surely noticed that Chris was missing. But if they noticed, and thought about it at all, they likely shrugged it off as a few minutes of tardiness—meeting with a teacher after class, a conversation with a friend in the corridor. Nothing more.

"Let me have your attention for a moment," Coach Fulton said.

Across the room, Mickey Ward was eyeing him closely.

The players turned in surprise.

"Chris won't be with us anymore," he said. "Chris is quitting the team for a reason that I am sure you will be able to understand."

Duddy Ford, suddenly back in place as the starting center, showed nothing. He stared evenly at Coach Fulton.

The other players frowned and exchanged glances.

"Last year, at Hall High in Indianapolis, Chris was involved in a tragic accident on the basketball court, and . . ."

On the practice court, Coach Fulton backed the Panthers away from the faster game that had worked so well with Chris's clothesline passes and his speed in getting down the court. The team went back to a more methodical style that took Duddy Ford's shortcomings into consideration.

For the players, the end of the faster style of play meant the removal of newfound fun. Hubie, Mark, and Marty loved racing down the court, taking in a pass, dribbling once, and laying the ball up. The others got a kick out of watching the play. For Alan, the return to the slower game meant fewer shots. Basketball is a game of ticking seconds—with only so many ticks to a game. Now the Panthers were taking more time getting themselves into position, leaving fewer ticks for Alan's shots.

One player, Duddy Ford, seemed relieved by the move back to a slower pace. Coach Fulton saw it in his face and was not surprised. He was tempted to say, "No, Duddy, we won't be expecting you to throw one-handed passes on a line half the length of the court. We know you can't do it. And no, we won't fast-break as often. We know you can't keep up with it." But, of course, he said nothing.

After the practice, a drill that underscored for all to see that Chris Patton was indeed gone, Bobby and Hubie were slow getting dressed. Finally, when they and Coach Fulton and Mickey were the only ones who remained, Bobby and Hubie approached Doug.

Hubie gave Bobby a sideways glance. Clearly, Bobby was going to do the talking. Hubie was standing by to offer support.

"Yes?" Coach Fulton asked, with a glance across the room at Mickey. The student manager had his back turned and was busy with his last duties. He was paying no attention to the two players approaching the coach.

Bobby's face took on the angry scowl that Coach Fulton had seen before on occasion. "He can't quit," Bobby said. "We need him." Bobby bit off each word and, at the finish, clamped his mouth shut and glared at Coach Fulton, waiting.

Coach Fulton glanced at Hubie. His face a blank, Hubie nodded slightly, as if encouraging the coach to agree with Bobby. Then Coach Fulton looked back at Bobby. He said, "Yes, and yes," and tried to smile.

"What?"

"Yes, Chris can quit. He certainly can, and he's done it. And yes, we do need him. No doubt about it."

Mickey, in the background, kept his back turned. Surely he was hearing every word spoken, yet he was obviously determined to stay out of the conversation.

"He's a quitter, that's what," Bobby snapped. "Just a quitter."

Coach Fulton felt his own anger flare. He glanced quickly at Mickey again. The student manager might not stay out of the conversation with his good friend being called a quitter. But Mickey continued his work, his back turned to them. Coach Fulton looked back at Bobby. He did not want Bobby making those kinds of statements to the other players, to the other students in the corridors, perhaps even to Chris Patton himself.

Then the coach leaned in slightly toward the boy and, speaking softly and as calmly as he could, said, "Bobby, I appreciate your concern and interest. I share your disappointment. But this is Chris's decision and we all—all of us, you understand?—are going to respect it." Then he turned to Hubie and said, "Right, Hubie?"

The other boy nodded his head and said quietly, "Okay."

Coach Fulton looked back at Bobby and waited.

"He's still a quitter, leaving us in the lurch," Bobby said.

"I don't want to hear that again—not from you, and not from someone who says they heard you say it."

The boy said nothing, and finally Hubie said, "C'mon, Bobby."

Coach Fulton said, "Okay, Bobby?"

"All right."

When they left, Coach Fulton looked across at Mickey, who had now turned around. "What do you think?" the coach asked.

Mickey shrugged. "He'll cool off. He always does."

In his apartment, Coach Fulton tossed his raincoat over the back of a chair, absently riffled through the mail that he had retrieved from the mailbox, and then picked up the telephone and the phone book and carried them across to a chair. He sat down, thumbed through the directory, found the number he wanted, and dialed.

Skip Turner was still at the radio station and quickly came on the line with a brisk, "Turner here."

"This is Doug Fulton, Skip. I forgot to call you when Chris Patton suddenly turned out to join the team. But I'm not forgetting to call you this time. Chris has quit the team."

"Quit? Why?"

Coach Fulton felt a rush of impatience with the broadcaster. Skip knew about Chris's background, and he had been there, at the scorer's table with his microphone, when the Barrington player bounced off

Chris and hit his head on the floor, and then lay there unmoving. Skip had seen what happened, and he surely saw how Chris reacted. But all Coach Fulton said was, "It was the accident during the Barrington game. It hit Chris hard. You know the reason."

"Sure I do," Skip snapped. "But that collision is no reason to quit. It wasn't even Chris's fault."

"Well, Chris took it hard."

"I can't believe it. I saw Chris after the collision. The two of you walked over to the Barrington bench. The Barrington player was fine. He even went back into the game. Chris seemed all right to me."

"Well, he wasn't."

"When did he quit?"

"I learned of his decision after I got home last night. His father called me."

"Last night! Why didn't you call me then?"

Doug rolled his eyes to the ceiling. "I waited until I could tell the players at practice today."

There was a moment of silence. Apparently even Skip Turner could understand why Coach Fulton didn't want the whole town to find out before the players knew. Skip said, "You've talked to Chris?"

"Yes."

"What did he say?"

"Nothing, and all I said was that I understood his feelings."

Again, silence on the line. Then Skip said, "What about you?"

"What do you mean, what about me?"

"Chris Patton is important to the team. What do you think about losing him?"

"Oh, I see. You can quote me as saying that we will miss him tremendously, not only because he is a great player but because he is a fine young man. Okay?"

"Okay, nice statement. Thanks for calling. Let me know if anything develops."

As far as Skip Turner was concerned, that was the end of the interview. Doug could almost see him bracing for the run to the microphone to deliver his bulletin to the world of Hamilton. But Coach Fulton said, "Wait a minute, Skip."

"What?"

"I'm trusting you to handle this the right way when you go on the air. I took you and George Holman into my confidence that night at Rudley's, and I don't want to be sorry I did. We're talking about a boy's life here. I want you to handle this thing the right way."

Skip was silent for a moment. Then he said, "I will. But I can't ignore it. It's news when the best player on the team quits."

"Yes," Coach Fulton said with a sigh, "I'm sure it is."

Doug hung up the telephone but kept his hand on the receiver, thinking. Then he picked up the directory and looked up the Pattons' home phone number, then dialed.

Brian, Doug. I've just spoken to Skip Turner at radio station, and I'm about to call George man at the *Post*. They may be calling Chris for a ment. I'm afraid that Chris's quitting is news, here's nothing we can do about it. I just wanted you know that they may be calling."

mm. Okay. Thanks for calling."

w's Chris?"

's all right. He seems more worried about letwn the team than anything else."

ach Fulton silently wished that Bobby Hogan een listening in on the conversation. Then he "Tell Chris that I spoke with the players before ice today, and everyone understands."

will. Thanks."

hen Coach Fulton called George Holman at e.

By the time Coach Fulton arrived at Hamilton h the next morning, everyone in the school—and obably everyone in town—knew that Chris Patton d quit the team. And they knew, in a vague way, omething about why.

Skip Turner had wasted no time in getting on e air with his bulletin, as Doug learned barely a ninute after talking with George Holman. He had eplaced the telephone on the desk and was walking toward the kitchen to prepare dinner when the phone rang. He turned and answered it.

"Skip Turner just announced that Chris has quit

the team," Mary Corliss had said. "He quoted you
I suppose you knew this was coming."

"Yeah. I called him just a few minutes ago
told him." Then Doug had frowned. He wishe
had turned on his own radio. "What did he say?

"Just that Chris had quit, for personal rea
related to the accident during the Barrington
game. He alluded to a previous accident but
give any of the details."

"Sounds okay."

Then earlier today, while pouring milk ov
breakfast cereal, Coach Fulton heard Skip T
say much the same thing again in the stat
morning newscast. Skip had finished by repo
that Chris's father had issued a brief statement
ing that his son made the decision on his own
personal reasons that had nothing to do
Hamilton High, Coach Fulton, or the team.

Doug had heard the broadcast again on his
radio while driving to the school, and now in the c
ridors he heard the chatter. A lot of the students
passed in the hall looked at him as if they wanted
ask a question, but none did.

On impulse, just before the bell for the first class
Doug turned and climbed the stairs to the secon
floor, heading for the classroom where Mr. Emerson'
English composition class met—Chris Patton's first
class of the day.

He and Chris arrived at the door together. The
boy was clearly surprised, and then his expression

changed to one of concern. Was Coach Fulton here
try to change his decision?

Coach Fulton smiled easily at Chris and said, "I
just wanted to tell you that you're going to get a lot of
questions today. Don't let 'em get you down. We're
all—the players and I—on your side. Remember
that."

Chris nodded and said, "Thanks," then walked
into the classroom.

Doug turned to head for his first-period gym
class and found that his meeting with Chris had
drawn an audience of gaping faces. He grinned at the
students, said, "Good morning," and walked away.

CHAPTER 15

The Wednesday drill went better than Coach Fulton had expected. The players seemed to unite around Duddy, determined to elevate the level of their own play and, with it, the level of Duddy's. As for Duddy, he seemed to have resolved to run harder and concentrate more, to make the big plays and commit no errors.

So when the Panthers took the court against the visiting Newcastle Falcons on Thursday evening, Coach Fulton took a deep breath, acknowledged that things could be worse, and recalled the adage often quoted by his college coach: "If you don't think you can win every time you play, you've got no business in the game."

* * *

During the team's pregame warm-up shots, Doug found himself scanning the crowd in the bleachers. Was Chris Patton here? No, if he were, he would not be in the bleachers, seated among people who would recognize him. That would attract too much attention, and Chris Patton would never put himself in that kind of spotlight. He would be standing at the end of the bleachers, if he was here at all. More likely, he wasn't. Coach Fulton glanced around but did not see him.

He saw Skip Turner at his table on the perch above the bleachers, his mouth working furiously, telling those not fortunate enough to be in attendance why the Panthers' game with the Newcastle High Falcons was important. Undoubtedly Skip, like a lot of the fans filling the gymnasium, was doing a lot of talking about Chris Patton, as well as Duddy Ford.

Then suddenly Coach Fulton found himself surrounded by his team at the bench.

The game was about to begin.

Doug extended both hands into the circle of players and joined in clasping and pumping three times. He looked at Duddy Ford. Was Duddy going to be able to carry over the determination from practice to the game? A lot was riding on his performance—for the team and for Duddy himself. He was playing in place of the great Chris Patton, and everyone knew it. Surely Duddy knew it, too. Coach Fulton looked at

Bobby, Alan, Marty, and Hubie. They were all going to miss the lift that Chris gave his teammates. Bobby was wearing an expression of intense determination. Well, maybe that was good.

They broke the handclasp, and the five starters moved onto the court while Coach Fulton and the other players sat down on the bench.

Duddy's opponent for the center jump was tall and angular, an inch or so taller than Duddy. In Coach Fulton's book, that meant simply that Duddy had to outjump him an inch or so. But Duddy wasn't used to being the shorter jumper, and he was eyeing his taller opponent with a look of concern.

The referee spun the ball into the air and Duddy sprang up after it. He beat the taller boy and tipped the ball to his left, to Bobby.

Coach Fulton leaned forward, elbows on his knees, and watched. Maybe Duddy's success was a good omen.

Bobby dribbled a couple of steps, then passed to Alan while Duddy ran to take up his position under the basket.

Alan bounced the ball to Duddy. Duddy faked to his left, fooling the tall player guarding him, then stepped forward, dribbled once, and went up, hooking the ball into the basket with his right hand.

A roar from the crowd broke the deathly silence. It was as if all the fans were holding their breath when Duddy went up, and now they shouted as much in relief as in delight at his success.

Duddy, running the length of the court to defend the Panthers' basket, was smiling. It was a nervous smile, revealing the enormous relief he felt in making good on the shot. It was not a smile of triumph.

Okay, thought Coach Fulton. Go ahead and smile, Duddy. That was an important basket. If ever a basket should inspire confidence, that was the one. Now, just keep on earning that smile.

But not ten seconds later, a fancy-dribbling guard wearing the white and blue of Newcastle High tied Duddy in knots with a couple of expert shoulder fakes, dribbled around him, and laid the ball up for a score.

Straightening himself on the bench, Coach Fulton feared that Duddy Ford had had his moment, and the game was going to be a terribly long one.

At halftime the Panthers led, 29–28, thanks in large measure to Alan Woodley's unerring accuracy from the outside. The Falcons unmercifully zeroed in on Duddy, which was fair enough. Duddy was the Panthers' weak spot on defense, and the Falcons knew it. Time and again, they drove through him to score. Duddy scored six points in the first half but had no more reasons to smile. Fortunately, Alan answered a lot of the Falcons' driving field goals with scoring shots of his own. But Duddy obviously was tiring, and the game still had a second half to go.

In the dressing room, Coach Fulton let the players breathe for a few minutes. He knew that every one of them was comparing his first-half performance with what might have been. With Chris at center, the Panthers would be standing ten or twelve points in the lead, ready to pull away in the second half. That was more fun than a one-point lead.

The coach stepped into the center of the floor. This was no time for a pep talk. Everyone was playing hard. So he ticked off a list of technical points.

To Duddy: "You're committing yourself too quickly under the basket on defense. It's leaving you vulnerable to fakes. Lay back. Give it a beat. Watch the guard perform his fakes. Then go after him."

To Marty: "You're passing up shots in the left corner that you ought to be taking. The player guarding you in that zone is lousy on defense. He loafs. Make him regret it."

He told Hubie to get under the basket more and help Duddy, told Bobby to keep feeding the ball to Alan, and told Alan—with a grin—"When in doubt, shoot."

And to all of them: "You've heard me say this before. The first few minutes of the second half are critical. More games are won in those few minutes of a good run opening the second half than in the last minute of the game. So go out there and take charge."

But neither the Panthers nor the Falcons took charge and made a run in the opening minutes of the second half. Instead, they traded points—field goals and free throws—and took turns with the occasional steal, fumble, and interception.

Coach Fulton found it difficult to keep himself in his seat on the bench. He wanted to stand, to shout, to exhort his team, as each goal seemed to him to be the one that was going to win the game. But he managed to stay in his seat, leaning forward, elbows on his knees, hands clenched.

With just under a minute and a half remaining in the game—and with the Falcons leading, 46–45—neither team had held more than a three-point lead. The lead had changed hands so many times that Coach Fulton had lost count. He repeatedly caught himself turning to look up at the scoreboard. Were the Panthers out front or trailing?

He called a time-out.

"Okay?" he asked Duddy.

Duddy nodded without speaking.

Duddy was drenched with perspiration and breathing heavily. He had driven himself hard all the way, with some success but also with a lot of failure. He obviously was worn-out. He had four fouls against him, and a tired player was more likely to foul.

Coach Fulton looked around at the other players. "If we take the lead, go into a full-court press. They're used to seeing us drop back beyond the center stripe to set up our defense, giving them a leisurely trip up the court. Pounce on them right away and press all the way. It should knock them off stride."

He paused to let the point sink in on the players. The Panthers usually played a half-court defense. But they had worked in practice on pressing their defense over the entire court, in order to be ready when the need arose.

"Then, if we get the ball and are still in the lead, slow the game down to a crawl. But keep an eye on the shot clock. We don't want to lose the ball because of a mental error. When it's running down, get the ball to Alan." He looked at Duddy. "If Alan misses, be careful not to foul going for the rebound."

Duddy was nodding his head, still puffing.

The time-out period ended.

Bobby threw the ball in to Alan. Alan dribbled in place for a moment until a Newcastle guard came out to harass him. Then he passed the ball back to Bobby. Bobby dribbled across the court, dropping the ball off to Alan, who then threw it back. Bobby fired the ball to Marty in the forward court. Marty dribbled twice, into the corner. Then he shot and scored.

The Hamilton High fans filling the bleachers roared, and Coach Fulton instinctively turned his head and glanced at the scoreboard.

The scoreboard flickered: Panthers 47, Visitors 46.

The Panthers applied a full-court press. It knocked the Falcons off their pace for a few seconds. With the clock ticking, the Falcons got across the midcourt stripe.

Bobby then stole the ball from a Newcastle dribbler, and with Alan, Hubie, and Bobby weaving out near the center stripe the Panthers ran down the clock.

With five seconds left, Hubie passed to Alan, and Bobby shouted, "Shoot!"

Alan tried to escape a tenacious Newcastle guard. He couldn't do it, but he let fly an off-balance shot just as the buzzer sounded. The ball missed everything—rim and backboard—and fell to the floor.

It didn't matter, and Bobby laughed and ran over to slap Alan on the back.

Coach Fulton stood up at the sound of the buzzer, glanced across the scorer's table at the Newcastle bench, and then walked down the sideline. He shook the hand of the Falcons' coach, mumbled something, and walked toward the dressing room. This was, he thought, a tough way to win a ballgame.

In the dressing room, he made the rounds of the players, patting them on the back, saying, "Nice game," and "Good going."

But he did not feel like the game had been nice, nor the going good, and neither did the players. Bobby's laugh of relief on the court at Alan's miss at the buzzer was the only and last expression of victory. There were tougher teams than the Newcastle Falcons in the Spoon River Conference still to come, and a one-point victory in this game did not foretell smooth sailing for the front-running Panthers, and the players knew it. They stripped off their uniforms in silence and headed for the showers. Coach Fulton perched himself on the training table and waited for them to emerge, towel off, dress, and depart.

When the last two players to leave—Marty and Alan—had let the dressing room door swing shut behind them, Coach Fulton found himself staring into the serious face of Mickey Ward.

"What is it?" Coach Fulton asked, almost absently.

"I think I've got it."

"Got what?"

"I told you that I was going to give Chris's problem some thought, and I think I've got the solution."

Without thinking, Coach Fulton glanced at the dressing room door. The door was closed, and no one was there. He said, "What's that, Mickey?"

"It's the guy who was injured."

Coach Fulton watched Mickey and frowned. "What about him?"

"He holds the answer."

"How's that?"

"I'll bet Chris hasn't talked to him since right after it happened. The guy was from Muncie, and that's a long way from Indianapolis."

"So?"

"Well, Chris has been worrying and suffering all this time. . . ."

"Yes." Doug was becoming interested now.

Mickey took a breath. "The way I see it," he said,

"that guy could clear up a lot of Chris's problem. He could tell Chris that he, not Chris, was out of position, which is true, and that it was an accident that could have happened to anyone, which is also true."

"Yes."

Mickey took a breath, then continued. "Why, if everybody thought like Chris, nobody in the whole world would be playing basketball, because it's been proven that a player might get hit in the eye and injured."

Coach Fulton gave a little nod, letting the thought settle in his mind.

"The injured player could tell Chris that. Don't you see?"

Coach Fulton smiled at the student manager's intense expression. "Mickey, you may be a genius, or you may be just crazy," he said. "Let me sleep on the idea."

While shaving the next morning, Coach Fulton looked at himself in the mirror and decided that Mickey was right.

Halfway from his car in the parking lot to the back door of the school, Doug Fulton heard the shout—"Coach!" He knew the caller was Mickey before he turned. The student manager was waving and then he broke into a little jog. Coach Fulton waved back and stopped to wait for him.

Mickey was puffing as he pulled up even with Coach Fulton. "You slept on it," he said without preamble.

Together they walked toward the door to the school building.

"Yes."

"And?"

They reached the door. Coach Fulton held it open for Mickey, and then followed him into the corridor. They stopped inside the door.

"I've decided that you're right," Coach Fulton said. "The boy probably could convince Chris."

Mickey smiled and nodded with satisfaction. "Good," he announced. "I'll talk to Chris."

Coach Fulton watched Mickey for a moment without speaking.

Mickey picked up on the thoughts racing around in the coach's mind. "Who did you think should be talking to Chris? Who, if not me?"

"Frankly, I had thought his father might talk to him. Or perhaps I would do it myself. But . . ." He let the sentence trail off. Mickey might, once again, be right.

"Look," Mickey said, pressing his point. "Chris and I are friends. I can talk to him. Then he can do what he wants." Mickey paused to take a breath. "You're always talking about not pressuring Chris. Well, I'm the only one who can talk to him without applying pressure. You can't, you're the coach. Even his father—well, his father's an adult, you know."

Coach Fulton nodded and could not resist a small smile at Mickey's reason for disqualifying Brian Patton. Then he said, "I think you're right."

"I've given—"

"I know, I know," Coach Fulton said with another smile. "You've given this some thought."

"Yes, I have."

The warning bell rang.

"Just one thing," Coach Fulton said. "Wait until I've cleared this with Chris's father. If his parents

147

approve, okay. But if not, nobody—including you—is going to meddle. Understood?"

"Sure, but they'll go for it. He wants to play, and they want him to play. It'll work."

"But wait until I tell you I've got the go-ahead. Right?"

"Yes."

"Now you've got to go," Coach Fulton said with a grin. "You've already gotten the only tardy excuse from me that you'll ever see."

"Umm." Mickey gave a little nod and walked down the corridor.

Brian Patton was skeptical. The fact was written all over his face. He was seated behind his desk, watching Doug and waiting.

Coach Fulton, taking a seat in the padded chair across the desk, felt a distinct discomfort. He had noticed the cool tone, the reluctant acceptance, when he telephoned Brian Patton to ask for a meeting. And now, when he had been ushered into the office, he noticed with a bit of a shock that Mr. Patton addressed him as Coach Fulton, not the familiar Doug he had adopted so quickly in their first meeting. Maybe Brian expected to be called Mr. Patton.

Coach Fulton wished he had explained more on the telephone, smoothing the way for this session. As it was, Doug was sure he was facing a father expecting to be told that the team needed his son, no matter the cost. And for sure, Brian Patton was ready to issue an instant rejection.

Coach Fulton took a deep breath. He started to ask, "How is Chris?" Maybe the pleasantry would thaw the atmosphere. But then he changed his mind. That would sound foolish. After all, Doug saw Chris in the corridors of Hamilton High two or three times every day, and it was clear how Chris was faring. He always said, "Hi, coach," with the same expression— the sad beginnings of a frown. His voice had no life, no laughter, in it. Doug could imagine Chris's mixed feelings. Chris wanted to play, wanted very much to play. But he could not stand to play. Yes, Doug knew how Chris was.

"I haven't much time," Mr. Patton said.

"I understand. I appreciate your agreeing to see me. I have an idea that might help Chris, and I wanted to discuss it with you."

Brian Patton said nothing, and Doug was sure he could read the thought going through the other man's mind: And beneficial to you, Coach Fulton.

Doug went on. "The first time we met, here in this office, you told me that you wanted Chris to return to basketball, that you thought it would be the best thing for him, that it would help him erase the memory of the accident."

"I remember."

"Do you still feel that way?"

"I'm not at all sure that I do. But I will listen to you."

In one of those weird quirks of the mind, Coach Fulton recalled a basketball game in his junior year of high school. His team was trailing by one point with seven seconds left, and the players were gathered around the coach at the sideline during a timeout. The coach told the players, "Get the ball to Doug." Then he turned to Doug and said, "And you shoot—and make it." This conversation with Brian Patton was turning out to be tougher than that shot. But he plunged ahead. After all, he did make that shot and win the game.

"Chris has immense potential, far beyond anything at Hamilton High. I'm afraid that if he lets that potential slip by, unrealized, he's going to regret it in later years."

"I've had that thought myself. Go on."

Coach Fulton put aside Brian Patton's statement that he did not have much time to spare. Chris was his son. Of course he had time to discuss him.

"Mickey Ward—you know Mickey—wants to suggest to Chris that he call the boy who was injured. What was his name?"

"Hartwell. Jimmy Hartwell." Brian Patton frowned at Coach Fulton. "Chris call him? To what purpose?"

"I understood from both Coach Barnes and you that neither the Hartwell boy nor his parents blamed Chris for the accident. If it was anyone's fault, really it was Jimmy Hartwell's. And the boy's parents were very sympathetic to what Chris was going through— all the guilt feelings, blaming himself, and quitting basketball at Hall High."

"Yes, that's correct. But I don't see—"

"Mickey's idea—and I think he's got a good point—is that Jimmy Hartwell can convince Chris that, yes, he was injured, but it was an accident—a one-in-a-million accident—and that it wasn't Chris's fault, and that he, Jimmy, has recovered. Then, maybe, Chris will be able to put the whole thing in perspective. He'll never forget, for sure, but maybe he'll be able to handle it."

Mr. Patton watched Coach Fulton without speaking.

Coach Fulton waited.

"No pressure," Mr. Patton said.

"No pressure," Coach Fulton said. "Mickey will make the suggestion to Chris, and then it will be Chris's decision whether to call Jimmy Hartwell. And if he does call him, it will be Chris's decision on whether to rejoin the basketball team. All of it will be in Chris's hands, and no pressure."

"That's important," Mr. Patton said.

"Yes," Coach Fulton said. "As a matter of fact, Mickey suggested that he—not you or me—talk to Chris for that very reason, and I think he's right. My talking to Chris could be construed as pressure. Chris might even see your talking to him as pressure from his father, who thinks he should play. But

Mickey is a friend, his own age. They can talk."

Mr. Patton stared past Coach Fulton for a moment. Then, speaking almost as if to himself, he said, "I don't suppose it would hurt to make the suggestion, and it wouldn't hurt for Chris to talk to the boy. I'm sure Chris's mother would agree." He turned to Coach Fulton and said, "All right."

Back at the school, Coach Fulton met Mickey coming out of his last class of the day and walked with him to the dressing room.

"I spoke with Mr. Patton, and he's agreed to your talking to Chris."

Mickey nodded. "Good. I knew Mr. Patton would think it was a good idea."

Coach Fulton reflected that Mr. Patton never said he thought it was a good idea. He just agreed to go along with it. But to Mickey, he said, "Mr. Patton also mentioned that there must be no pressure."

Mickey gave out an exasperated sigh and said, "Look, I know how to handle this."

Doug grinned and had to agree that Mickey probably did.

The rain began that evening, just after Coach Fulton reached his apartment. He stood for a moment at the living room window, overlooking the apartment building's parking lot, and watched the rain come splashing down. It looked like one of those rains that was going to be around awhile. The thought crossed his mind, as it had before, that a basketball coach, for all his problems, had it over a football coach when it came to the weather. Basketball was played indoors, away from the rain and the cold. He never could think of any other advantage.

The telephone rang, and he turned from the window and walked across to answer it.

Surely it could not be Mickey with a report on a conversation with Chris. The coach and the student

153

manager had left the dressing room together after practice. Coach Fulton had arrived home only minutes ago. Mickey, despite living only a block from the school, could hardly have been home more than a few minutes.

Doug picked up the telephone.

"Anything new?" snapped Skip Turner.

"New? No."

Skip let the answer hang, as if expecting Coach Fulton to turn himself around and make some sort of announcement. In the moment of silence, Doug felt a sudden sense of alarm. Did Skip Turner know something? Skip had never called him at home at night. The sportscaster dropped in on practice on occasion and sometimes stayed around to talk later. But he never had had a reason to call Coach Fulton at home. So why now? Surely Brian Patton, even if he were called by Skip, would not have told him about the meeting in his office. But maybe Skip, by coincidence, had seen the Panthers' basketball coach entering or leaving the Gould building. If Skip knew that Brian Patton's office was there, he could put two and two together and decide that calling Coach Fulton might be a good idea. And, really scary, what if Skip went on the air with some half-baked story about Coach Fulton meeting with Chris Patton's father?

"On Chris Patton," Skip said.

Coach Fulton quickly weighed the odds and said, "He hasn't come back to the team, if that's what you mean. You could have seen for yourself at practice today."

"How'd practice go?"

"Good. The boys probably thought it was hard. But it was good."

"No chance, huh?"

"No chance what?" Coach Fulton asked innocently.

"Chris Patton."

"Nothing that I know of."

"Just a hunch." Then he added, "Wishful thinking, maybe."

"I can join you in that."

"You'll call me if anything breaks?"

"Sure."

Doug hung up the phone and turned back to the window. The rain was still streaming down in the darkness. He wondered when Mickey would be talking to Chris. Maybe he was at Chris's house now. Or maybe Chris was at Mickey's house. Or they were out somewhere together. And he wondered when and if Chris would call Jimmy Hartwell. And then, when and what Chris would decide.

Then he turned from the window and walked into the kitchenette, deciding on a salad and a bowl of soup for dinner on this rainy Friday evening.

On Saturday morning, the rain continued.

Coach Fulton had the athlete's dislike of rain. In good weather he liked to spend his Saturday mornings on the tennis court or the golf course. Frequently on wintry Saturday mornings he and Otis Humphrey met at the YMCA and played handball.

But he had made no date with the football coach today. With a rematch with the tough Bakerville Spartans coming up on Monday night—and with Chris Patton gone from the team—Coach Fulton had been tinkering for three days with the possibility of calling a special practice on Saturday morning. He knew one theory of coaching held that exhausting practice sessions made the game itself seem like a breeze to the players. But Doug never bought that theory. He thought that playing basketball, whether in practice or a game, should be fun, not a grueling ordeal to be endured. Practice was necessary to hone the skills, perfect the teamwork, and master the plays; it was not an instrument for turning fun into drudgery. In the changed situation, his team could use more drilling, for sure. But he feared he was on the edge of making the game of basketball a drudgery, especially after the long and hard practice on Friday. So in the end Coach Fulton had put down the temptation to run his Panthers through one more drill to prepare for Bakerville.

Instead he gathered up dirty laundry, dumped it in the washer, and left the machine to its work.

He walked into the living room, stared at the telephone a moment, and gave a little jump of surprise when it rang.

Mickey's voice said, "Coach?"

"Yes, Mickey. Have you spoken with Chris?"

"No, not yet."

Coach Fulton waited.

"But I called Jimmy Hartwell this morning, and—"

"You what?"

"Called Jimmy Hartwell," Mickey repeated. "Before talking to Chris, I wanted to be sure that everything was going to go the right way."

"Mickey."

"Huh?"

Coach Fulton rolled his eyes in the moment of silence. Once again, he could see the adult Mickey Ward, a lawyer, arranging everything to "go the right way." Coach Fulton said only, "Never mind. What did Jimmy have to say?"

"You're not going to believe it."

"Try me."

"Jimmy's back playing basketball."

Coach Fulton blinked at the telephone. For a moment, he didn't speak. Thoughts raced through his mind. The first one was disbelief. Mickey must have misunderstood.

Finally, he spoke. "Jimmy Hartwell is back playing with his high school team?"

"Well, no, not that," Mickey said. "But he's playing in a Saturday morning league at the YMCA." He paused. "Same thing, really. He's playing the game, don't you see?"

"Maybe," Coach Fulton said, trying to sort out his thoughts. One told him to direct Mickey to call Chris right away and tell him. Then a second thought stopped him. There was something wrong in that idea. He waited for Mickey to continue.

"He was a bench-warmer on the high school team and never got into games much anyway; when he did he always found himself up against much better players. That's how he got hurt by Chris. He made a mistake. He told me this himself. In the Y league, he gets to play, and he's playing against others of his own caliber."

Coach Fulton nodded to himself without speaking. He understood what Jimmy Hartwell was doing. Coach Fulton had known players of marginal ability in both high school and college who came to the same decision. They were boys who loved basketball but lacked the skills or physical attributes to be really good players. Although they might have made the squad, they were destined to sit on the bench. So they chose intramural basketball and logged all the playing time they wanted. But Coach Fulton had never known one who did it after an accident that came close to leaving him blind.

"Now," Mickey continued without waiting for the coach to comment, "I've given this some thought."

Coach Fulton grinned. Mickey certainly had given the matter some thought. And it seemed that when Mickey gave something some thought, he was usually worth listening to. The coach said, "And what have you concluded?"

"I'm not going to tell Chris about this."

Coach Fulton thought he saw where Mickey's reasoning was heading.

"To tell Chris that Jimmy Hartwell is back playing basketball and that Chris is afraid to play—well, talk about pressure. It would be like calling Chris a coward and daring him to play."

"I think you're right. You make the suggestion to Chris, and let him take it from there."

In the afternoon, Coach Fulton sat slumped back on the sofa, his feet up on the coffee table, and watched North Carolina defeat Duke on television, while the rain outside continued.

But at the finish he couldn't remember anything about the game.

When he flicked off the set, he walked to the telephone and dialed. Mary Corliss answered.

"Do you ever go out to dinner on rainy Saturday nights?"

"Sometimes, when invited."

"I'll pick you up about six. Okay?"

"Fine."

Maybe, he thought, Mary's company would make him forget some of the troublesome questions in his mind, at least for a while. What if Chris decides against calling Jimmy Hartwell? Should Mickey or should I then tell him that the boy is playing basketball? And if so, then what?

Watching the Bakerville Spartans taking their warm-up shots, Coach Fulton thought the big center named Johnson looked even larger than he had remembered from their previous meeting. In that first encounter, Chris had defeated Johnson, outrebounding and outsmarting him. And because Johnson's four fouls sent him to the bench midway through the second half, Chris had also outlasted him.

But on this Monday night there was no Chris Patton in the Hamilton High Panthers' lineup.

Maybe, thought Coach Fulton, that was why Johnson seemed to loom even larger than before. The Panthers were going to face him with Duddy Ford, who was a little shorter and a lot slower than Chris. He was also lacking the fierce competitive drive that Chris brought to the game.

Coach Fulton turned his attention from the Spartans to his own Panthers warming up at the other end of the court.

Alan Woodley hit one from fifteen feet out. Well, he was going to have to hit a lot of them tonight, Coach Fulton thought, if we're going to have a chance.

Doug shifted his gaze to Duddy. He had the ball under the basket. With a deep frown of concentration on his face, he dribbled once, turned, went up, and hooked the ball into the basket.

Then Coach Fulton absently focused on a spot on the wall beyond Duddy. The center and all the other players faded into a fuzzy blur as he relived the past day and a half.

A few minutes after noon on Sunday, Mickey Ward had called to tell him: "Chris says he'll think about it."

Then all through Sunday afternoon and evening and finally bedtime—nothing.

He had woken up this morning, dressed, eaten breakfast, and headed for the school, with the start of the Bakerville Spartans' game only about ten hours away—and still nothing.

Once during the morning he passed Mickey in the corridor. He knew that his face was asking a question, and Mickey answered with only a shrug and a small shake of his head.

And once he met Chris in the corridor between classes. His face did not ask a question this time—

Doug made sure of that—and he said only, "Good morning, Chris." Chris replied, "Hi, coach." That was all. Nothing more.

At noon, he saw Chris and Mickey and two other boys—boys he knew by name and face only from gym class—eating lunch together in the cafeteria. It wasn't likely the foursome was discussing a telephone call to a boy named Jimmy Hartwell. He walked on, unnoticed by Chris or Mickey.

In the late afternoon, during the free hours between the end of the last class and the time when the players would gather in the dressing room, he toyed with the idea of telephoning Brian Patton. The temptation was strong to ask if Chris had made the call. But in the end he fought off the temptation. There really was nothing to do but wait.

When Mickey arrived in the dressing room a few minutes before six o'clock to prepare for the game, Coach Fulton was waiting for him.

"Any word?" he asked.

"Nothing. Chris hasn't mentioned it, and neither have I."

"Okay," the coach said in a tone of resignation.

"You said it was Chris's decision. You said not to pressure him."

"I know, and you're doing the right thing by leaving him alone to make up his mind."

The players began arriving—first Alan Woodley, then Bobby and Hubie, and then Duddy, followed by the others.

Coach Fulton walked out to await the arrival of the Bakerville team bus. He always tried to meet the visiting team and show the coach and the players to their dressing room. Walking past the open doors to the basketball court, he saw Mr. Hodges, Hamilton High's chief custodian, giving the floor a final sweep with a wide push broom. Just inside the door to the building, the ticket takers were setting up for the evening's work. A few early fans were arriving.

He stood outside in the chilly darkness only a few minutes before the red-and-white bus bearing the Bakerville Spartans pulled into the lot.

As he walked toward it, Coach Fulton wondered what Chris Patton was doing at this particular moment.

The players were returning to the bench for the final seconds before the start of the game. Coach Fulton took a step forward to meet them at the sideline.

The crowd filling the bleacher seats on both sides of the court let out a roar as the referee walked to the center circle with a ball under his arm to await the players for the opening tip.

The Bakerville fans who had driven the twenty miles to watch their Spartans were seated together in the bleacher seats across the court from the benches. They were easily identifiable, with their red sweaters, shirts, and jackets.

The other seats were a wave of green and gold,

crowded with the fans of the Panthers. With or without Chris Patton, the Panthers were at the top of the Spoon River Conference standings on this night.

Coach Fulton extended his hands for the team clasp. They pumped—once, twice, three times—and released. The five starters moved onto the court, and the others, along with their coach, sat down on the bench.

Across the scorer's table, at the Bakerville High bench, Coach Adrian Blake was standing at the sideline calling out something to a player, who was nodding.

In the center circle, Duddy and Johnson braced for the leap. Duddy's face wore a grim look of determination.

The referee spun the ball into the air.

Duddy and Johnson went up.

Johnson easily beat Duddy and tipped the ball to his left, to one of the Bakerville guards, who dribbled in place while the methodical Spartans moved into position for their first attack on the basket. Duddy turned and ran to the basket to take up the defense. Johnson ran with him.

On the bench, Coach Fulton watched without moving. He recalled that Chris, too, had lost the opening jump to Johnson.

Dribbling and passing, the Spartans weaved around at the center stripe. Then one of the guards, taking a pass near the foul line, faked a move to his left, dribbled right, and headed for the basket. Johnson turned and effectively screened Duddy out of the play. The Spartan guard dribbled through and laid up the ball. It dropped through.

Coach Fulton took a deep breath and instinctively glanced at the scoreboard: Panthers 0, Visitors 2.

Bobby Hogan flipped the ball inbounds to Alan Woodley while the Spartans dropped back to set up their half-court defense. Alan dribbled unhindered to the center stripe, then passed back to Bobby. Bobby dribbled across the center stripe, angling toward the sideline. He fired a pass down the sideline to Marty Townsend. Marty took in the pass, turned, shot— and *swoosh*. The score was tied.

Coach Fulton first noticed the sign of something new on the face of Bobby Hogan. Usually laughing and relaxed on the court during a game, Bobby wore an expression of intense determination, almost a threatening anger. When he passed to Marty, his jaw was thrust out in defiance—defying Marty to muff the pass, defying him to miss the shot. Bobby had been angry about Chris's defection, and he was angry now.

And when he shot, Marty fired the ball with an authority born out of a concentration that he did not always display. Marty seemed not so much angry— Marty seldom was angry—as simply determined.

The other players, too, were wearing expressions of rock-hard intensity.

Even Duddy, now on defense shadowing Johnson under the basket, was working harder than he ever had worked before.

From the bench, it seemed to Coach Fulton that his players had decided to win without Chris Patton. There had been no big pep talk. He knew of no meeting of the players without him. No, it seemed simply that each of them, alone, had decided the team was going to beat the Bakerville Spartans without Chris Patton.

Coach Fulton felt a small surge of hope. A team determined to win just might do it.

The Spartans, however, had other thoughts—and they had Johnson. He beat Duddy on the first three rebounds. But Coach Fulton had to credit Duddy with making the larger boy stretch himself to win. If Duddy kept pressing, he was going to win some of the rebounds.

Alan Woodley missed his first two outside shots and, when the second one bounded off the rim, looked to be on the verge of tears. Alan knew, surely, that his scoring from the outside was crucial if the Panthers were going to stay in the game.

Coach Fulton got to his feet and stepped to the sideline, calling out to Alan, "Okay, okay. Next time. Next time."

Alan heard him and nodded grimly.

Then, as if making up for the two misses, Alan promptly intercepted a pass at midcourt. He fired the ball to Bobby and moved forward. Bobby returned it to Alan. Alan shot, sending the ball through the basket without touching the rim.

The scoreboard read: Panthers 9, Visitors 13.

The two teams battled through the next minutes, exchanging field goals. The Panthers pulled within two points twice, but they were never able to make the necessary connections to move into the lead. Johnson was the dominating factor on the boards, and Duddy, no matter how hard he tried, did not have the size, timing, or the feather-touch tip-in skills of Chris Patton. And those were the ingredients needed to beat Johnson. Alan's outside shooting and Bobby's lay-ups kept the Panthers within reaching distance of the Spartans on the scoreboard. But the Panthers seemed unable to make the additional surge needed to take the lead.

With less than a minute left in the half, Johnson leaped and caught a high pass over Duddy, turned, and placed the ball in the basket to extend the Spartans' lead to seven, 27–20.

Coach Fulton stood, stepped to the sideline, and signaled to Bobby, who was inbounding to Alan. Bobby nodded an acknowledgment and called the play as Alan dribbled to the center stripe: Hold the ball for a last-second shot by Alan. If he succeeded, the Panthers would go into the dressing room trailing by five—not as good as being in the lead, certainly, but still in the game.

It came as no surprise to Coach Fulton that Coach Blake was on his feet at the sideline, shouting something. He had guessed the Panthers' tactics, and the Spartans moved out from their half-court defense to challenge Alan and Bobby and to try to bottle up Alan.

Coach Fulton stepped back and sat down.

Alan, facing two defenders at midcourt, passed to Bobby. Bobby dribbled in place, letting the seconds tick off the clock, until a Bakerville defender came after him. Then he passed down the sideline to Hubie Willis, who fired the ball back to Bobby. Alan ran around one of his defenders, using him as a screen to block out the other one, and broke into the open.

Bobby fired a two-handed pass to Alan.

The last seconds were ticking away.

Alan shot and scored.

The buzzer sounded with the score 27–22.

Coach Fulton and the players on the bench stood up and began the walk to the dressing room. "Five points down," Doug said, glancing at the scoreboard. He saw Skip Turner in his broadcast booth above the bleachers, speaking into a microphone. He wondered if Chris Patton was somewhere in the crowd. Probably not. He wondered if Chris was listening to Skip's broadcast, hearing his own name mentioned as part of the problem the Panthers were having with the Bakerville Spartans. No, probably Chris wasn't listening.

Coach Fulton began to frame in his mind what he was going to say to the players—the comments, criticisms, suggestions, compliments. He realized that, although they were trailing, he had more compliments than criticisms to hand out. The Panthers were playing tough-minded basketball, playing their best. That was all he ever asked.

At the door leading out of the gym, he stepped aside and let the players go through first. Then he followed them into the corridor and across to the door of the dressing room.

He pushed open the dressing room door and stepped in.

There, in uniform, seated on a bench, surrounded by staring players, was Chris Patton.

Chris looked up at Coach Fulton. "I got it worked out," he said softly.

Coach Fulton watched him a moment. Then he asked, "Are you sure?"

Chris nodded slightly, returning the coach's gaze. "Absolutely."

None of the players said anything. They all were staring in a dumbfounded way, first at Chris, then at Doug. Coach Fulton would have guessed that Chris's surprise reappearance would have sparked shouts of welcome, grins all around, an enthusiastic cheer about what they were going to do to the Bakerville Spartans in the second half. But there was only blank-faced silence from all of them.

Perhaps the players, like Coach Fulton, were at first too stunned to think, and then wondered whether Chris really had, as he said, "got it worked out."

"Okay," Coach Fulton said finally. "You'll start the second half. Welcome back."

Chris grinned.

At that moment, Mickey Ward entered, having completed his routine halftime task of stopping at the scorer's table to get the first-half statistics on both teams for Coach Fulton's review.

Mickey stopped, stared at Chris for a moment, and then said with a straight face, "It's about time."

Chris turned to Mickey and said, "Sorry I was late."

Their exchange had the effect of relieving the astonishment, wiping out any doubts, erasing the puzzlement.

Fittingly, Duddy was the first to approach Chris. He simply shook his hand, saying nothing. Then Bobby Hogan, frowning, but now more in wonder than anger, stepped across and slapped hands with Chris. And then Hubie Willis and the others, all smiles, were patting Chris on the shoulder, jabbing his arm, or shaking his hand.

Coach Fulton turned to Mickey. "Go tell Skip Turner that Chris is back and will play the second half. He'd never forgive me if we just walked onto the court with Chris."

Mickey nodded and left.

"Now," Coach Fulton said, "we're down five points against a good team, and we've got some work to do."

171

* * *

The Panthers returned to the gym, crossing the corridor from the dressing room and passing through the door onto the court in single file. Chris, in the middle of the line of ten players, gave a smile and a nod to Coach Fulton, holding the door, as he passed him. He mouthed something without making a sound and was gone before Coach Fulton realized he had said, "Thanks."

The first Hamilton High player to appear on the court started a cheer from the crowd, as always, and the noise increased as the other fans realized the team was returning.

By the time Coach Fulton followed the last player through the door, Chris was crossing the court.

The crowd was slow to recognize that there was one more player with the Panthers, and that the player was Chris Patton.

Then an enormous roar rolled down from the bleachers on both sides of the court and grew louder still when Chris picked up one of the basketballs bounced onto the court by Mickey, dribbled a couple of times, and took a shot at the basket. His shot missed. But the roaring cheers continued.

Coach Fulton walked across the court to the bench. He paused and watched for a moment. Then he stepped to the scorer's table and advised the scorer that Chris Patton would be starting the second half. He glanced at the Bakerville bench and saw

Coach Blake staring at Chris. Then Coach Blake looked at Coach Fulton. Coach Fulton gave a little nod, and Coach Blake nodded in return.

Yes, Coach Fulton thought, the big center named Johnson has his work cut out for him. This time, at least, his team has a five-point head start over the team led by Chris Patton.

Walking back to the bench, Doug glanced at the crowd in the bleachers. Surely Mr. and Mrs. Patton were there somewhere. But he didn't spot them and finally turned his attention to his players taking their warm-up shots.

He stood at the sideline, arms folded over his chest, oblivious to the roaring cheers filling the gym, and watched Chris. He was leaping up and plucking a missed shot off the backboard with both hands. He came down, dribbled out a couple of steps, stopped, turned, shot, and hit the basket. He smiled as he moved forward to recover the ball. Chris Patton was the perfect picture of a boy loving to play the game, reveling in his exceptional talent.

But what about when he collided with someone?

The second half was four minutes old when the Panthers took the lead. A tip-in by Chris had narrowed the difference to three points, 27–24. A shot from the side by Marty Townsend cut it to one, 27–26. Then Johnson wriggled away from Chris and put the ball in the basket, returning the Spartans to a three-point lead, 29–26. Alan Woodley responded with a lay-up, and Chris hit a fifteen-foot jumper to put the Panthers out front, 30–29.

The Panthers' first lead of the game brought another roar from the crowd as the Spartans put the ball back into play.

Coach Fulton found it difficult to maintain his motionless pose on the bench. He wanted to stand up and cheer with the fans when Chris's fifteen-footer put the Panthers in the lead. And now, with the Spartans' guard dribbling toward the center stripe and the Panthers falling back into their defensive positions, he wanted to leap to the sideline and implore his players to recapture the ball—steal it in mid-dribble, intercept a pass, bat the ball away from someone—and score. He settled for leaning forward, elbows on knees, hands clasped tightly.

Crossing the center stripe, the Bakerville guard turned and flipped a one-handed pass to his partner at the sideline.

Suddenly Bobby, as if acting on Coach Fulton's silent signal, appeared out of nowhere. He lunged forward and took in the ball on his fingertips. He bounced the ball out in front, chased it, caught up with it, dribbled twice, and went up, laying the ball in the basket.

By the time the ball dropped softly through the net, Coach Fulton was on his feet. So was everyone else in the gym, with a roar of a cheer.

From there, the two teams settled into swapping

field goals. The Panthers stayed out in front, but only barely, with a lead ranging from one to three points. Neither team was able to break away in a decisive run.

But Coach Fulton was counting something in addition to points. He watched Chris on the defensive backboard working against Johnson, and then watched Chris on the offensive backboard. Chris was winning two of every three battles for the ball on the backboard. On defense, he was coming down with the ball held in both hands, looking for a teammate to receive a pass. And on offense, he was beating Johnson to the ball and repeatedly giving the ball a fingertip brushing, enough to tip it into the basket. A frustrated Johnson fouled Chris twice.

Yes, the teams were swapping field goals, and the score remained close; but Coach Fulton knew that Chris's dominance on the backboards was giving the Panthers an edge that was going to pay off—and, maybe, put Johnson in foul trouble. Time was on the side of the Panthers.

Coach Blake, possibly seeing the situation the same way Coach Fulton saw it, called a time-out with five minutes remaining and the Panthers leading by four points, 48–44.

Coach Fulton stood up to greet the five perspiring players walking off the court toward him.

With the players gathered in a semicircle in front of him, Doug gave them the only advice he had to offer. "Put the ball up more often, go ahead and

175

shoot. Chris is beating their center on the boards two out of three times. The odds are that we're going to get a second try on a missed shot."

When play resumed, the Spartans began moving in help for Johnson under the boards. One or the other of the forwards joined him, in effect double-teaming Chris. The space under the basket was crowded.

On a leap for a rebound, the three of them—Chris, Johnson, and the second Bakerville player, went up together. Johnson threw a hip into Chris, and the referee's whistle screeched. The impact knocked Chris into the other player and they both hit the floor with a cracking sound.

Coach Fulton was on his feet and at the sideline in a single bound. Was Chris hurt? Was the other boy hurt? He wanted to see Chris get up. He wanted to see the other boy get up. And, he realized with a heart-stopping horror, he wanted to see Chris's face. What was Chris thinking?

Chris got up quickly, rubbing his right elbow and flexing his arm. No trouble there. The Bakerville player got to his hands and knees, then stood up. He was shaking his head like a groggy fighter. He had taken a head bump on the hard floor.

Chris walked across and patted the player on the shoulder.

Coach Fulton resumed breathing and returned to his seat on the bench.

Chris made his free throw, stretching the Panthers' lead to seven points, 55–48, with a little less than three minutes remaining.

Finally, Coach Fulton sat up straight, crossed his legs, and enjoyed the remaining minutes of basketball.

The final score was 61–50.

The players and Coach Fulton had to almost shove their way through the crowd to get to the dressing room. Once inside, Doug closed the door and locked it. He hadn't seen anything like this since his college team won its way into the final sixteen of the NCAA tournament—all the family members, all those fans nobody had seen before, all those reporters. In this situation tonight, a lot of the people were fans who wanted to cheer the dramatic comeback victory. But a lot of them simply wanted to hear the story of Chris's return.

Coach Fulton turned from the closed door and faced his players. Then he grinned and raised his arms, fists clenched, and said, "Beautiful."

Bobby shouted something that sounded like "Yow!" and laughed.

Then the dam burst, and everyone was shouting and laughing. Chris kept mussing Alan's hair, and Alan, for once, was grinning. Hubie was pumping a fist in the air.

There was a knocking on the door—hard bangs, one after another in a quick staccato.

Coach Fulton unlocked the door and opened it a

crack. He found himself facing Skip Turner. Behind Skip, the corridor was crowded with people.

"Let me in," Skip demanded.

"In a few minutes," Coach Fulton said.

"My audience—"

"Your audience will wait."

Then, beyond Skip, he saw Brian Patton's face. He gestured to him, and Chris's father came forward. Coach Fulton opened the door wide enough to allow Mr. Patton to slip into the dressing room while at the same time stepping in front of Skip, blocking him. Then he backed into the dressing room and closed the door, locking it in Skip's indignant face.

Mr. Patton walked across to the grinning Chris and extended his hand. They shook. Then father and son hugged. Stepping back, they looked at each other, as if this was a moment they both wanted to record.

Brian Patton turned and stepped out of the group of players, stopping next to Coach Fulton.

Mickey bustled by, gave Chris a slap on the back, then went about tending to his business, seemingly oblivious to the shouting and laughter filling the room.

Mr. Patton leaned forward and said to the student manager, "I don't know what you said, but it was the right thing."

Coach Fulton smiled and said, "He gave it some thought." Mickey glanced at Doug quizzically, then nodded his acknowledgment to Mr. Patton and walked on.

"I can't wait to talk to you," Coach Fulton said.

"There isn't much to tell. Chris did call Jimmy Hartwell—this afternoon, when he got home from school. He told his mother what he was doing. Chris and the Hartwell boy talked for a long time. And afterward, Chris stayed in his room until dinner. He was in there when I got home, and his mother told me what had happened. At dinner, he didn't say anything, just picked at his food. His mother and I exchanged a lot of glances and tried to keep a conversation going. After dinner, he went back into his room for a few minutes, then came out and asked me to drive him to the school. I said, 'Are you sure?' He said, 'Yes.' And that was it. We arrived during the first half."

Coach Fulton took a deep breath and exhaled, watching the players whooping it up without making the first move to take off their uniforms and head for the showers.

"There was one other thing," Mr. Patton said. "On the way over here, Chris asked if I thought you would let him come back. I told him I thought you would."

Coach Fulton turned and grinned at Chris's father.

He looked back at the shouting players. "I've got to get these boys in the showers, and then I've got to let Skip Turner in."

He moved toward the players, and Bobby Hogan cried out, "Let's win the state championship!"

"Before you win the state championship," Coach Fulton said with a grin, "you'd better shower. And then, you know, there is the little matter of the rest of our schedule. The Chandler Cougars are coming up again on Thursday night, for example."

The players began undressing, and Brian Patton said, "I'll wait for Chris outside."

Coach Fulton nodded, unlocked the door, and opened it. Mr. Patton slipped through the opening into the crowd.

"C'mon in, Skip," Coach Fulton said. As the angry newscaster stepped inside the dressing room, Doug told him, "The players had earned a private moment."

Skip ignored the explanation and asked, "Where's Chris Patton?"

Coach Fulton grinned at him and said, "In the showers."